DARK FALLEN DAYS

By Nicholas Peluso

D1716881

Chapter 1

September, 1940

"Some say these are the end times. Some say this is needed for us to find our faith again. War is a last resort when diplomacy fails. We are God's children, and if we fail, so does hope, and hope is all we have left. Without it, we have turned our backs on God. All we need to do is choose. Choose to ask for peace, forgiveness, tolerance, and mercy. If we don't ask for them, then we don't believe, which is the greatest travesty of all. These dark days will pass because we have chosen hope." Silence as Father Scott turned from his congregation. A muffled cough and a baby crying broke the silence at St. Joseph's Catholic Church in Toms River, New Jersey.

Before the communion portion of the mass, Father Scott led the risen congregation in the "Our Father." While the prayer was said, Paul looked down and to his right at the exposed ankle of Mrs. Thatcher. Paul, being only eight years old, was fixated on the exposed body part of Mrs. Thatcher. Only in her late twenties, she was not unfamiliar with glances from the opposite sex but never one so young. She adjusted her dress so it dropped to cover much of the ankle. A large hand fell on Paul's left shoulder, startling him. Jack Phy wanted his son to pay attention to mass and join the prayer.

The sun was still up after Sunday mass, and Jack decided to work on his 1938 Ford Coupe. He fiddled under the hood, dressed in an undershirt and some old, brown work slacks. Jack was a mechanic at the local filling station and was considered by most men in town a wizard regarding combustion engines.

"Best way to learn is to take it all apart and put it back together again." Jack would tell his son Paul.

"No better grease monkey in all of Toms River than your father, Paul." Tom Parker, an elderly regular customer, would tell Paul whenever he saw Jack's son in the corner station. The women in Toms River also noticed Jack and wanted to know more about him besides the fact that he was a mechanic and widowed. One thing the single ladies in town noticed about Jack was that he frequented the Ocean House Pub most weeknights and weekends. Women look for tells, which was a big bad tell for Jack. Jack's wife, Nancy, passed away while giving birth to Paul. She was a slight woman, and four days in labor took their toll on her. The funeral was only attended by immediate family. Jack never even told his cousins that he was married. They were a quiet couple that kept mostly to themselves, earning them the nickname around town as the "Quiet Phy Family."

While Jack was tightening bolts down on the Coupe's engine, Paul was sitting on the front lawn in play clothes. Cut off jeans, a white undershirt, and barefoot. Paul liked the feel of the grass under his feet which was still damp from last night's rain. He was pulling up clumps of crabgrass and tossing them aside.

"Paulie, what are you doing?" Jack asked.

"Nothing. Thinking."

"About?"

"Will I die like an ant? Will I die like Mom did?" Paul looked at his father in the driveway. Jack's head comes out from under the hood of the car.

"I suppose I should be honest with you now that you're getting older. Yes, we will die one day, but that won't be for a long time. Just keep a keen eye and always be wary of your surroundings. That's why I tell you to look both ways before crossing the street and never talk to strangers." Jack says.

Jack went back under the hood of the car. Paul was not upset by what his father had said. Instead, he smiled, not so much on the outside but inside. Paul imagined himself getting older and what he might look like and be like. He looked forward to driving and having the townspeople treat him with respect, like his father. Paul also wondered how big he would be and if he would grow up strong enough to kill his father like he kills ants in the yard.

After dinner with a full stomach of steak and string peas, Paul is drowsy as he lays tucked in bed for the night. The only illumination in the room comes from the moonlight peeking through a tiny space between the curtains. Pictures of elephants, lions, tigers, and monkeys on them. No pictures of birds. Paul didn't like birds. The quick, jerky movements, long wing spans, and the way they would swoop down and attack scared him. One bird attack happened as he was cutting through the baseball field behind his school. Paul would walk home and cut through the backwoods behind the field. He knew not to go alone, but he enjoyed the alone time going to and from school. The squirrels and raccoons he would see filled him with joy. Paul liked animals and could not wait to get a slingshot to start collecting them.

Mrs. Miller was trying to teach third-grade math to her class. Paul sat in the back and looked out the classroom window, and drifted off into imagination. The teacher's words become soft and muted as he looks out at the slight change of color in the leaves on the trees that surround the baseball field. Paul imagined all the animals in the woods and wished he could be out playing with them, gathering them, and keeping them.

"Paul, eyes forward, please." Mrs. Miller says.

Paul did so alertly at the sound of his name being called. Mrs. Miller had long black hair and blue eyes behind her glasses. Out of all the adults, Paul knew she was the only one who did not wear a cross around her neck. Paul was fascinated by his teacher for reasons he did not fully understand yet. He found her slim body and sharp features pretty. Her soft voice as she explained a lesson to him over his shoulder felt soothing and gave him an erection.

"She's Jewish," Ralph said to Paul as he swung his strapped school books over his shoulder.

"What's that?" Paul asked as he followed Ralph in the hallway.

"My dad said they killed Jesus," Ralph said, pushing his glasses back up the bridge of his nose. Ralph was sweating from the September heat and the fact that he was overweight. Unusual for a child this young to be overweight in a summer town so close to the beaches and parks of the New Jersey shore.

"Mrs. Miller didn't kill anyone," Paul said, shrugging his shoulders. He liked Mrs. Miller, but now he was more curious about her.

"I killed a bullfrog last week with my slingshot. I got it for my birthday." Ralph said, looking at Paul's face for a reaction. Ralph wanted to see a little jealousy in Paul, a strange desire for an eight-year-old.

"Did you keep it?" Paul asked.

"The frog? Eww, gross, no. You're weird, Paulie."

The two continued outside the school and through the baseball field to the backwoods home.

"We can shoot something this weekend if you want," Ralph asked.

"I don't know. I'll see if my dad will let me go."

"Ok, let me know," Ralph said, hoping Paul would come along.

Ralph didn't have many friends, so when an opportunity presented itself for someone to play with, he took it. Ralph went up the three wooden steps of his front porch. The smell of Ralph's mother's cooking made Paul's stomach ache for food. Paul lived two houses down. Mrs. Kinsley, the old librarian, lived between them. She would sometimes admonish Ralph and Paul if they made too much noise in front of her house playing stickball. Paul sat on his front steps and took the books off his shoulder. He sat quietly, listening to the wind rustling the leaves in the trees. He heard a dog barking down the street. He watched the postman deliver mail from house to house across the way. All the while, he was thinking of one thing, using a slingshot to kill something.

Jack's Ford pulled into the driveway. Paul hopped off the step with his books and got in the front seat of his father's car.

"Slam the door hard, Paulie. Don't need you flying out into the street." Jack said, and Paul closed the door as hard as he could.

Jack always took Paul to work with him after school let out. One of the advantages or disadvantages of Paul's mother being gone was the amount of time he had to spend with his father. Today Jack was happy to have some company. Work had been slow. Jack enjoyed watching Paul come out of his shell more. For a while, Jack was worried that Paul was too quiet, especially after his mother's death. The quietness of his child sometimes made Jack feel uneasy.

"How was school?" Jack asked.

"Mrs. Miller is a Jew," Paul said, and Jack was taken aback by the blunt statement.

"How do you know about stuff like that?" Jack asked, puzzled.

"Ralph told me. Did Jews kill Jesus?"

"I don't like you boys talking about that. You're too young for that kind of talk."

Paul put his head down, partly ashamed but partly proud of himself for knowing something only adults knew.

The traffic and work had been steady but slow at the corner station on Water Street and Main. Most filled up their gas tanks on Friday for the Indian summer weekend.

"You know the rules, Paul. Just watch and learn. Don't touch anything. One day this will be how you earn a living." Jack told his son. Paul watches his father do two oil changes, change a flat tire, and even do an engine pull.

"It's hard work. This is how you will get a nice house of your own. Find a wife and even have your own kids. You earn, you never take. Nobody gives you anything. Earn. Say it."

"Earn," Paul said. Paul forced a smile as he met his father's stare. Paul thought a little about the garage but not about having a family of his own. He was still too young, and those things seemed way off in the future. All Paul wanted to do was use a slingshot with Ralph.

Jack felt the need to teach his son life lessons as early and as often as he could. He knew his son was too young to be stuck in the garage at work all day. Paul should be outside playing baseball, riding his bicycle, and just be a kid. Jack felt sorry for his son. A boy growing up without his mother is like a boat without a sail. If Jack died tomorrow, then no one would care for his son. Those thoughts kept Jack up at night.

Saturday morning was crisp with a light breeze. The sun shone particularly bright as it bounced and danced off the dew on the grass. Ralph's mother, Mrs. Post, watched Ralph and Paul play in the backyard through the kitchen window. She glances up now and again and watches them play tag as she is doing a crossword puzzle. She saw Ralph dart from behind an oak tree and slap Paul's left shoulder.

"You're it!" Ralph said, out of breath. Paul couldn't believe Ralph had caught up to him.

Paul knew he was much faster than Ralph, but it was Ralph's backyard, and he knew it better. Both boys tried to catch their breath with their hands on their knees.

"When can we use the slingshot?" Paul asked.

"I don't know. My mom keeps watching us. Sometimes she takes a nap in the mornings after breakfast."

Mrs. Post did nap most of Saturday mornings. She was portly, and like Ralph, she would snore at night as the fat around her neck cut off her air supply. The momentary lack of oxygen and choking would cause her to wake every ten to fifteen minutes. To make up for the sleep lost during the week, she would nap on Saturdays.

After three more games of tag and one game of hide and seek, Mrs. Post was out, but not before figuring that a six-letter word for complacent was apathy.

Ralph kept his slingshot in the garage, so that was where the boys were. They opened the garage door just enough for them to slip in. Spider crickets bounced out and gave Ralph a scare, and Paul laughed at him. Inside, the garage was dark and dank.

"Where do you keep it, Ralphie?"

"By my dad's fishing pole over here." Ralph led Paul to the left side of the garage, and behind a tackle box was the slingshot - a sturdy Y-shaped piece of wood with a thick rubber tube attached at the upper two ends.

"I'm only allowed to use it when my dad is around," Ralph said as both boys hurried out of the garage and shut the door behind them.

They went down the hill and into the woods that separated the houses from the school's baseball field. The woods were quiet and cooler than the backyard. The boys treaded light and soft to not startle any critters. Ralph held the slingshot but realized that Paul should be holding it.

"You shoot today. Just pull back as far as you can and release. You're going to miss it, but that's ok.

"I can do it. I'm not missing." Paul says. The two followed a beaten path in the woods. Overgrown stickers caught them as they walked through, but they didn't care. Being on the hunt was too much fun. More fun for Paul. Ralph hoped his mother didn't wake up early from her nap.

A few yellow leaves danced down in front of them. The two boys look up to see a squirrel dashing across a thick tree branch ten feet overhead. Paul gripped the slingshot and pulled back the rubber band with a small stone ready to fire.

"Yes. Get him, Paulie." Ralph whispered. The squirrel bounced down the tree, gripping it tightly with its claws. It stopped suddenly and looked at Paul.

"Pop him."

Paul calmly closed his left eye to focus his shot. The squirrel was frozen. Paul released the stone. In an instant, the squirrel fell with its tail spasming just over the brush. The spasms stopped.

"Wow, first shot!" Ralph said, smiling. He ran to the squirrel. Paul slowly followed behind.

The squirrel lay in a clump with its brains oozing out of the right eye Paul had shot out.

"Took me a week of practice before I hit anything. You're a natural." Ralph picked up a long branch and began to poke the squirrel's body. He felt it squish under the poking and prodding. Paul just watched and began to feel dizzy. Sweat started pouring down his forehead and the trees begin to spin around him like a kaleidoscope of green and brown.

"I got to go home. I don't feel too good." Paul hands Ralph the slingshot and turns to leave. He is swaying from side to side trying to catch his balance.

"You ok, Paulie?" Ralph asks, but there is no answer.

Under the quiet of night the only sounds coming from Paul's room are that of whimpering. Paul is crying for reasons that are not yet available to him. He in part is crying for the squirrel he killed and also for the realization that he had power over something. That kind of responsibility and the consequences that come from it are too much for him. The squirrel was alive and then it wasn't all because of him. Sure killing bugs was one thing, but to see blood and brains was something new and too real. Under the strain of holding back tears his breath started to come back and the tears that were on his cheeks dried. He was calm now.

"I'm never hurting anything again." Paul quietly told himself. He still wanted to collect animals, but not hurt them. He wanted to control them. Control was better than killing. These thoughts and desires are now in his head. The want or desire to kill had been pushed way back into his mind. Deep into his unconscious. The impulse to kill would never come out again. Perhaps it would with his offspring.

Chapter 2

April, 1979

Pensive or excited? Laura Krueger could not decide which. Her stomach churned as she sat in her beat up second hand Volkswagen parked in the lot of her part time job as a cashier at the local grocery store. It's her first job that she got last spring when she turned sixteen. The emotions she was feeling now were not from her job, but from a certain man who would come into the grocery store during her shift. He was tall, burly, clean shaven with salt and pepper hair. He had a nice smile. The only drawback as far as Laura could tell was his age. A man in his late forties should not be flirting with a teenage girl and this red flag should have been noticed by Laura. The attention was unwanted, inappropriate, and bordering on "creepy" as Laura's coworkers would tell her. To Laura it was all of those things, but it was also nice, new, and oddly enough, familiar. It reminded Laura of the way her father had doted on her when she was younger. Cancer in his blood ended all that ten years ago. His death was a closure. His suffering was the real heartbreak. It was a time and a feeling that Laura wants to forget. It was now only Laura and her mother. They did not spend much time together anymore with school and now the two of them are both working. Laura's mother worked double shifts at Toms River Community

Hospital as a nurse. Few friends didn't help Laura's loneliness either. She made acquaintances in school and at work, but nothing real. Laura ached for a boyfriend. Never having attention from boys made her self esteem plummet. She was skinny, pale, with stringy brown hair and no boys gave her a second look. So when Paul Phy, the salt and peppered hair gentleman smiled at her, it made her heart soar. Paul would always pick her line to check out the few groceries he would buy. When she saw him she would get butterflies in her stomach and put her head down.

"He's creepy, Laura. He's like stalking you. Only shows when you're on the floor. Buys the same things each time and only gets on your line. Plus he is super old. Like forty maybe even fifty." Sue says. Sue is one of Laura's work acquaintances. They talk from time to time if their breaks happen to match.

"What if he starts showing up at your house? Waiting for you after school?" Sue says as she flips through a gossip magazine. Laura stands by the doorway of the break room.

"He won't do that. He's just flirty. Like a big teddy bear." Laura says, twirling her hair looking down at her shoes.

"A pervy, old teddy bear." Sue adds under her breath.

The doubts were there as Laura recalls these past conversations with Sue. As Laura sits in her car, rain starts to fall. Not too much yet, just a few drops that ping off the metal roof of her car. The doubts subsided as anticipation took over. Having a relationship was uncharted territory for Laura and the thought of it was intoxicating. Kissing, holding hands, being intimate. To finally be seen and treated like a woman for the first time in her life. The taboo was also enticing. Sex with an older man. A much older man. Emotions all over the place are too much of an aphrodisiac for a teenage girl to resist.

Three hours into her shift and no sign of Paul Phy. Usual clientele, old ladies squeezing fruit in the produce section, housewives going up and down each aisle with a small child close behind. It was late in the afternoon, but it wasn't all that unusual to not see Paul. His visits came at different times during Laura's shift. He owns his own garage and can make his own hours. Laura begins twirling her hair as she waits by the cash register. Perhaps the rain earlier kept Paul away, Laura thinks. She thinks of other things too. Her future. She knew she didn't want to work long and thankless hours being a nurse like her mother. Blood and sickness also made Laura uneasy. Laura thought of maybe becoming a teacher. She enjoyed literature and children. She also loved poetry, but there wasn't much money in that and Laura had not seen enough of the world yet. She wanted to travel more. The tri-state area was not exactly fertile soil for a creative mind like Laura's. Eventually Laura would definitely like to have children. Preferably a girl. She wanted to mold a girl into someone strong, caring, outgoing, beautiful and popular. All the things Laura was not. She did want her future daughter to be kind and decent. Something the beautiful and popular girls at school were not. Most of all Laura wanted a daughter so she could have a best friend. Sit up all hours of the night and talk about anything from art, music, fashion, and boys at school. A best friend to confide in and share secrets. Laura did not want to be alone anymore.

Seven at night and Paul never showed. The first time he had not come to see Laura. A sinking feeling hits Laura in her chest. Thoughts of Paul losing interest in her or finding someone else made her heart ache. As Laura walks to her car a little more hurt sets in with each step she takes. The rain has stopped and the air is cool and this helps Laura breathe and relax for a moment. She reaches into her purse to find her keys when a hand grabs her right shoulder. She jumps and turns to see Paul smiling at her.

"Where were you today?" Laura asks. Paul just stares into Laura's eyes and pulls her into him for a long and much awaited kiss. She melts in his embrace and tastes his mouth. A warm tingle takes over her body and the ache in heart is gone. For the first time Laura feels love.

The first three months of Laura and Paul's relationship were bliss. Days and nights spent together. Nights if Laura could sneak out the house or if her mother happened to be scheduled for overnights. Paul really wanted to take Laura away to Atlantic City for the weekend, but that would be a tall order. There is no way Helen Krueger would let her only child out of her sight for an entire weekend.

"Completely inappropriate. You're too young to have a boyfriend." That was Helen's stance when Laura asked her permission to attend the high school dance the year prior. To go away for a weekend Laura would have to go around her mother. To do that she would have to lie and the lies got easier to tell each time she had to. The lies covered up late night trysts in Paul's truck, his shop, or even Paul's house. It was the same house Paul grew up in. Paul's father, Jack, passed away seven years ago. Paul missed his father terribly. Playing cards, drinking beers at the local pub, fishing off the piers and beaches of Seaside Heights and Seaside Park. The one and only silver lining was the gas station Paul took over. Paul had earned his apprenticeship there and handled the day to day operations as his father got older.

The heart attack happened in January of 1972. It was the morning after a snowfall. Ten inches had fallen and Jack decided to shovel out the front porch, the driveway and by the mailbox. The sun was out and temperatures were above freezing. This caused a layer of heavy slush under the snow. Just after nine that morning Jack was finishing up clearing around the mailbox when he felt an explosion in his chest. Paul hadn't noticed his father had fallen until a few minutes had passed. He came running. Ambulance came and took Jack to Community Hospital. He died just before eleven p.m. That was the saddest day in Paul's life. He was only a newborn when his mother died so this was his real first loss. Paul had not handled it well. The bottom of a beer bottle was all that Paul looked forward to. It helped mask the pain, but the pain would be right back when he sobered up. The quality of his work in the shop also slipped. Business started to taper off and most of Paul's longtime customers began to look elsewhere. The depression deepened. That was until a young cashier at the grocery store caught his eye.

Young, maybe too young. Young meant innocent, available, impressionable, possibly still a virgin. Virgin means clean. Virgin means tight. Paul became infatuated with this girl. Skinny, long nose, almost like a bird. A small bird that Paul could own. Finally something he could own. How to get her Paul didn't know. He remembered some things that his father told him about girls.

"Girls like compliments. Girls like to smile. Girls like security." Jack would tell Paul when he was a teenager. Paul never had much luck with girls in high school. After he graduated it was right to work in the garage. The only females he would see would be customers and most of them were married or too old. Paul had resigned himself to being a bachelor for life. It suited him. He was never much good at sharing or compromise. Those two key elements needed for any sort of worthwhile relationship to have a chance. Everything was about Paul. He was an only child. Jack's schedule revolved around Paul. Teachers in school took more time with Paul because he was slower than the other students. Paul would play up being slower than the others because he enjoyed the attention from female teachers. Mother figures. Paul's friends schedules had to change also to accommodate Paul's extra hours after school to catch up on lessons. Everything was about Paul and any future relationships with women also had to be about him.

The first time he saw Laura he quickly glanced down at her store name tag. Even her name was pleasant to him. He needed to know more about her. He introduced himself and made small talk about the weather. The first meeting for Laura was forgettable. The first meeting for

Paul was unforgettable. He lay awake at night thinking of things to say to her. He needed to know her schedule at the grocery. To know that he needed to do some research.

Paul knew Laura went to the local high school. Simple enough to follow her from school to her home in the southern part of Toms River. At around three in the afternoon she would leave home and go to work at the grocery store. It was a few miles from her home and Paul would stay at least four car lengths behind Laura's Volkswagen. She was never the wiser. Her shift ended at eight in the evening and Laura went directly home. Paul figured out quickly that Laura did not have a social life which also led him to believe she had few or no friends. He made mental notes while sitting in his pick up truck parked across the street from Laura's home. The Flamingos "I Only Have Eyes For You" is playing on the car radio.

The house is a dilapidated two story with white paint chipping. The front lawn had not been cut in weeks. Paul then knew the father was not in the picture. She was poor so no need for an elaborate date. A few dinners and a movie and she would be his. Her financial situation suited Paul just fine as his finances were dwindling.

Laura's bedroom light goes out at exactly ten.

"Early sleeper. Good night, angel." Paul says to himself, making another mental note.

Chapter 3

July, 1979

The Happy Hour Bar on the corner of Main Street and Magnolia was a small dive bar

whose patrons were older, blue collar men who were born and raised in town. Paul preferred it to

other bars for its small size and atmosphere. No loud music and no college kids. One reason in

particular that Paul liked the Happy Hour was a blonde haired, blue eyed bartender. Angela

Mallek was friendly and had a cute smile for everyone. She couldn't make a drink if she tried.

She was there to sling beer, smile, and keep the old timers coming in. Her being in her early

twenties helped. She was new in town. Only arrived a few months prior from Philadelphia. She

was a bookkeeper at a gentlemen's club, but for family reasons she relocated to Toms River.

Angela had a one year old son named Billy. She was proud to show off pictures of him to anyone

who took an interest. Billy had blue eyes and sharp features like his mother. Angela never talked

about Billy's father, so Paul assumed she was a single mother. Not that Paul would ever pursue

Angela. Paul was very much in love with Laura. He couldn't take Laura to the Happy Hour

because of her age. So every Friday night, if he could, he would admire Angela from afar. Most of the men's advances towards Angela were rebuffed. She would roll her eyes or make a self deprecating joke.

"You wouldn't want me. Damaged goods." Angela would say.

"Too much baggage, honey." Referring to her child at home. She tried, but the advances never really stopped. It wasn't often a single, blonde girl would be in the bar, so the men had to at least try. Angela was steadfast and never dated. Paul noticed that Angela seemed more interested in talking with a young, black girl that would come in right before closing. Tasha Higgins was her name. Paul would eavesdrop on their conversations if he was in earshot.

Tasha was just a few years older than Angela. The two shared a trailer two miles down off of Route 37. It was the three of them, Tasha, Angela, and Billy cramped into a two bedroom trailer. When Tasha came in the bar before closing there were some curious glances. There are not many black residents in this part of Toms River. Most lived in Lakewood, a town five miles north. Tasha didn't mind the glances, after all, she was a street wise girl from south Philly.

Tasha used to work part time at the same gentleman's club Angela did. That is where they met. Part time at the club and the other part time was in the streets. Tasha made decent money there, but not enough to satisfy her pimp Priest. Roy Higgins was his real name. He was Tasha's first cousin on her father's side. Tasha and Roy even went to the same high school in Philadelphia. Roy would introduce his friends to Tasha and for five dollars they could touch her breasts. Roy would give Tasha a small percentage of the money, of course, but if she ever told anyone in the family then Roy would be shipped down south to live with his grandmother. Roy's father, Tasha's uncle, was Louis Higgins. He was a Baptist preacher at the Tasker Street Baptist Church. Preacher Higgins was his name in that part of town, so people gave Roy the nickname Priest and it stuck. After both Roy and Tasha dropped out of high school they hit the streets hard.

Roy offered protection for local, poor, desperate girls trying to earn. His size afforded him that at being six foot seven inches tall and close to three hundred pounds, but solid not fat. He protected Tasha too and she in turn would recruit more girls. The money was good and Roy "Priest" Higgins was the biggest earning pimp in south Philly.

Tasha loved Priest, but feared him. If he ever suspected that she was slacking on the corner or skimming he wasn't afraid to slap Tasha or any girl around. He wouldn't hit hard enough to knock teeth out or leave any scars just in case a nurse in an emergency room asked too many questions. He also wanted the "Johns," street slang for customers, to pay top dollar and they wouldn't if the girl was busted up.

One night in December of last year Priest did go too rough with Tasha. The disagreement started over missing keys to a "John's" car. He wouldn't pay until Tasha returned the keys. Priest sided with him over his own cousin. It didn't help that Priest was coked up out of his mind. It wasn't uncommon for a girl to steal possessions off a "John" and sell it back on the street for any price. Watches, wallets, credit cards, and jewelry were the most common. Car keys didn't make much sense, but Priest assumed Tasha was up to no good.

When Tasha got to her apartment after midnight the place was a wreck. Priest had been throwing what he could get his hands on and flipping furniture looking for the missing keys.

"Where you been all night?! Where the goddamn keys at?!" Priest at the top of his lungs.

"What keys? What the fuck are you talking about? What did you do to my place motherfucker?!" Tasha taking in the wreckage.

"Lying, bitch. You lifted that fool's keys and you're going to flip his car ain't you? What's the matter? I don't pay you enough?" Priest isn't yelling, just cornering Tasha in the apartment using his size to intimidate her. Neighbors heard the fighting, but would never call the police on

Priest. The last good samaritan that did was found dead floating in the Delaware River.

"I didn't take anything. That fool was high and angry that I wouldn't suck his dick for five dollars. Now you need to back up." Tasha says. She could see the cocaine residue in Priest's nostrils.

"You a ho. You negotiate. You don't steal from the customers, otherwise they don't come back. You need to start using your fucking head." Priest says.

"I'm a working girl. I'm no whore. Now, again, you need to back the fuck up."

"Talking back." Priest forces a smile. He raises his arms up like a surrender and steps back. One step and Tasha can now breathe. The second step she let her guard down. There was no third step, only a backhand from Priest and a beating that almost knocked Tasha unconscious.

Tasha needed time off from the club to recover. They didn't sympathize and she lost her job. She couldn't afford to live on her own so she moved into Angela's apartment two blocks away. They had become close that year working together. Flirtatious glances while changing at the club. Tasha took pity on Angela having a newborn alone and having to work in a club just to support him. Tasha and a couple of other girls at the club would help watch Angela's baby while she worked. It started as a close friendship that was necessary because they were all they had. The friendship evolved into love. A deep love. They did their best to hide the relationship from Priest and the other girls. If word hit the street then customers might not want to pay top dollar for a lesbian. Angela didn't work the streets, but Tasha did. If Priest found out about Angela he would do whatever he could to exploit the relationship. He could threaten Angela and the baby's safety if Tasha didn't comply with his demands. It was too dangerous.

Tasha sat on the bed while Angela looked for clean clothes. Most of the wounds were superficial, not structural. No broken bones, but she could use some stitches on her scalp, mouth and back.

"Tired of this. I need to fix his evil ass." Tasha says through a busted lip.

"How would you? I mean we can't go to the cops. You can't just leave, he would find us and then he'd kill us." Angela says putting a t-shirt over Tasha's bruised back.

The two sit on the edge of the bed looking into each other's eyes. The silence is broken.

"I'll kill him." Tasha says.

Angela knows Tasha can't kill Priest. *The man is a giant, how would a skinny girl like Tasha even bruise Priest?* Angela thought.

"You can't kill him. I know you want to. It would take three men to hurt that man."

"Fuck it. I'll shoot him. Any man can die from a bullet." Tasha said through gritted teeth.

Tasha lays back down on the bed and stares at the cracked ceiling. Her eyes are unfocused and bouncing around. The thoughts are too many and jumping back and forth in her brain.

"If he dies and you're gone then everyone will know it was you who killed him." Angela says while nervously biting her fingernails.

"Can't hide the body. That mother fucker is too big. Can make it look like an overdose. Slip something in his stash. Goes up his nose and boils his brain." Tasha says while watching Angela get up and go to the window.

"His car is gone. What if we get someone to do it for us?" Angela says while looking down at the street through the window.

"Carmen. She has a brother who just got out at Rikers. They're close. He practically raised her. He has no idea she is turning tricks for Priest. Tony's got a temper and when he finds that shit out then..damn. Got ten years for assaulting an off duty cop. All I gotta do is tip him off and let nature take its course. After that we can go to Jersey." Tasha says while sitting up in bed.

"What if he doesn't kill Priest?" Angela says.

"Tony's temper is all I got." Tasha says.

A letter was written and addressed to Tony's grandmother's house. The letter was about Carmen and her current drama with a man named Priest. Tony's grandmother couldn't make sense of it so she handed the letter to Tony who was sitting on the sofa watching television. He bolted up and went to his bedroom.

"What is it, Tony? Is Carm in trouble?" Grandmother asked.

"I gotta go to Philly and take care of this." Tony said through the closed bedroom door.

As Tony changed his clothes certain words from the letter flashed in his mind. *CARMEN, HOOKING, BEAT, PIMP, PRIEST.* At the end of the letter is an address and an apartment number. Tony crams the letter in his back pocket and goes to the bedroom phone.

"Pick me up in an hour. You owe me. We're going to Philly tonight. I gotta straighten some punk out. Prison rules. No guns." Tony hangs up the phone.

The letter hinted at the size of Priest. Tasha was subtly giving Tony a heads up. The size of Priest was of no concern to Tony. Even at only five feet nine inches tall, Tony was a thick two hundred twenty pounds of all muscle. All he did in prison was lift. Nothing was going to stop Tony tonight. Carmen and his grandmother were all he had in the world. He would die to protect them. In the kitchen he took a steak knife and would later wrap some duct tape over the handle. Not only did the tape help with slippage it also could be removed leaving no fingerprints. Tony did not want to go back to prison, but for family he was willing to risk it. Carmen had moved to Philadelphia from New York to earn on the streets. She wouldn't dare do that in New York near her grandmother and Tony. In early 1977 she met Priest through a friend. From there she met

Tasha. The letter was not a total fabrication. Priest had hit on her in the past. Tasha had embellished some of the injuries. She had to. Tasha wanted a future with Angela away from the poison that was Priest. This letter and its consequences were her only hope of escape. Priest was her cousin and that part bothered Tasha, but she would have to reconcile those feelings in the future.

It was a four hour drive from Bedford Stuyvesant to south Philly. Tony was in the passenger seat and his friend Hector was driving. A four hour drive with two black men in a car and not once being pulled over was a feat in and of itself. The beat up Chevy was now parked down 16th Street. Hector was pensive. Tony was focused and waiting for any sign or hint of movement. All the lights in Priest's apartment building were out.

"Is he even here?" Hector asks.

Tony pays no mind and reaches for the knife under the passenger seat. He can see a large man in a blue suit and gold chains staggering towards the apartment building.

"That's one big drunk mother fucker." Hector says with eyes wide open.

"When I get in the building you start the car and wait for my ass. Don't bounce on me." Tony says with eyes fixed on Priest. Priest is now inside and Tony gets out of the car and walks with his head down and knife tucked under his jacket sleeve. Hector watches as Tony goes into an alley behind the building. Hector was anticipating at any moment red and blue lights flashing in the street, but so far no police were in sight. Two minutes pass and Hector is worried about his friend. Tony had saved Hector's life in Rikers after a card game dispute. Tony had to save Hector because they were cellmates. Tony didn't want to get mistaken for Hector and get a sharpened toothbrush in the eye. Hector listened to Tony. He was a leader, a boss, a friend.

Hector's heart nearly comes out of his chest as he sees Tony running out from the back of the apartment building covered in blood. He starts the car and knows Tony had done what he came to do. Tony had killed Roy "Priest" Higgins.

At about the time Priest took his last gurgled breath of blood and oxygen, Tasha, Angela, and Billy were on the I-95 in New Jersey headed east. No words were spoken, just quiet. A nervous quiet mixed with a sense of relief. Angela was driving while Tasha looked out the window and Billy was asleep in the baby seat in back.

"I can call Carmen tomorrow to find out if it's done." Tasha said.

The sign up ahead with silver lettering and a green background read FREEHOLD NEXT RIGHT. Angela glanced at it and glanced into the rearview mirror to see Billy sleeping

"Be in Toms River in less than an hour." Angela said.

Angela and Tasha didn't have much money so it would be tough at first to find a place to stay. Hotels, then maybe save enough for their own place. It was going to be tough, but not as tough as south Philadelphia had been to them.

Chapter 4

August, 1979

Paul has a date tonight. He is taking Laura to Island Heights. A one mile long boardwalk along the Toms River that leads out into Barnegat Bay. Some of the homes along the boardwalk are over one hundred years old and include widow watch decks on top. The view from the widow watch decks can see out across the river. Wives would stand and watch as their husbands would come into port. Some did not come back, hence the name.

It's a scenic spot for locals to unwind. Best of all, especially for Paul, it was free. He had picked Laura up from the grocery store and opened the car door for her like a gentleman. It was not instinct, it was merely rehearsed behavior Paul had seen in the movies and television. The talk on the ride over to the boardwalk was small and polite. Most of the conversation revolved around Laura's life, not Paul's. Laura knew very little of Paul. She had just assumed he was shy and guarded. She knew of his job, some of his family backstory and the Happy Hour Bar he liked to spend some evenings. His mailman would know as much. One part of his personality that Laura didn't like was that Paul liked to put down other people. The week prior they passed by a bad car accident on Route 9.

"Dumb asses. Serves them right." Paul said.

Laura felt uneasy. He could be cold and distant sometimes. Laura would brush these off as eccentricities. She did love him. He was kind and attentive to her. She looked forward to their dates even if they were a little frugal. Walks were nice, but some nights were chilly. Fishing on his canoe was fun too, but a dinner in a restaurant would be a nice change of pace. Laura would feel guilty. She was nitpicking. She felt lucky to have any man's attention. Paul did have his own home. The one he had inherited. Very little of the home was updated. It almost reminded Laura of her grandparent's home. On the mantle over the fireplace were baby pictures of himself which Laura found odd. The only current items in the home were a television set and a couch. The house was clean, freshly painted, and the lawn was trimmed. She had imagined living there.

Laura felt she was getting ahead of herself as she sat in the car at Island Heights. The two had yet to even officially be boyfriend and girlfriend. The thought of being in a relationship made her glow. It would be her first and she hoped it would be her last.

Paul felt he had confided a lot to Laura. She knew about his family, his job, where he lived and where he liked to spend his free time. It was more than he had shared with anyone. Paul was happy with Laura and he wanted to cement the relationship with her. They had fooled around a little, but never went all the way. The only way to truly cement the relationship in Paul's opinion was sex. Paul was hoping tonight would be the night.

It was humid tonight, even on the bay. The two sat in Paul's truck and looked out at the moonlight dancing on the ripples of the water.

"You look good tonight, babe." Paul said.

"Thanks. You look nice too."

"Been thinking about us. Where things are going. Where I would like them to go. Do you think about that?" Paul asks.

"Sure. Of course." Laura says shyly.

Laura felt giddy that Paul was thinking of a future together. She couldn't help her smile.

"Where do you see us in a year?" Laura asks.

A pause as Paul ponders the question. He knows a wrong answer will kill any chance for sex tonight, so he says what he feels Laura wants to hear.

"Us living together."

That is exactly what Laura wanted to hear Paul say. The emotions in Laura were too much and all she could think to do was hug Paul as hard as she could.

"Oh, Paul, I love you so much."

"You're my girl. I have to do right by you." Paul says.

Paul had Laura right where he wanted her. They kissed deeply and Paul knew he was getting laid tonight.

Helen Krueger did not approve of her daughter, Laura, being out all hours of the night. She was a teenager with responsibilities. Partying, drinking, getting high, or God knows what else with boys was strictly forbidden. The long hours at the hospital may be to blame. Maybe the lack of communication between mother and daughter could be the fault of Laura's father's death. Raising a teenager by herself was tough for Helen. Laura needed to spread her wings and have experiences to find herself. Helen wanted Laura to be her little girl for just a bit longer, but it was fruitless. Rebelling and a push for independence was inevitable. Helen loved her daughter dearly and knew Laura was not attractive. *Laura, plain and tall*. That's what Helen would think. She would also think that a boy would only pay attention to Laura if they were getting something in return. The thought of Laura being sexually active made her blood boil. A lack of proper religious education growing up may have been a mistake. The thoughts and second guesses made Helen crazy as she sat on the couch in the living room waiting for her daughter to come home.

"Where are you?" Helen said softly, while thinking of calling the police.

The lovemaking had been rougher than Laura had expected. Once they got to Paul's home he had pushed her up against the wall and shoved his tongue deep into her mouth. His hands groped and fumbled under her blouse until he got to her breasts and squeezed. He pressed his crotch against hers. She had trouble breathing the stubble from his face scratched her cheeks. Laura was not enjoying this in the least. He was like a big child touching a girl for the first time. Paul picked her up and carried her to the bedroom.

"Maybe we should slow down a bit." She says as Paul lays her down on the bed. She scoots back a little.

"Been too long. Take your clothes off." Paul says.

Paul unbuttons his pants and Laura begins to undress. She had thought of leaving, but was afraid of rejecting Paul right now. There was nothing romantic or passionate about his sex. Thrusting, kissing, groping. His penis was large, but Laura was not wet so it was even more uncomfortable when he was inside. As Paul was on top of her thrusting his hips into her Laura couldn't wait for this to be over. Five minutes later it was. Paul rolls over sweating.

"Awesome, babe."

Just then a panic sets in. She realizes now with the wetness between her legs that Paul had not worn a rubber. Laura is now in a cold sweat and gets up to go to the bathroom.

"You ok?"

Inside the bathroom Laura checks at her swollen and red opening. Paul had ejaculated in her and Laura was furious.

"Why didn't you wear protection?" She shouts through the bathroom door.

"What are you talking about? We're a couple. Couples don't do that." Paul says.

Laura cleans herself up with a washcloth. She sits on the toilet and forces herself to urinate and push out Paul's mess. The thought of her getting pregnant was too much for Laura. Her mother would kill her. She gets up and washes her hands and face and looks at herself in the bathroom mirror.

"Stupid, stupid, stupid."

Laura leaves the bathroom and sits on the edge of Paul's bed.

"You ready for round two?"

"What if I get pregnant?"

"You won't get pregnant. It takes a bunch of times to get pregnant."

"No it doesn't. One time can. Why would you think that?" Laura asks.

"You're getting worked up for nothing, babe. Relax and come here." He says patting the spot next to him on the bed.

Laura reluctantly gets next to Paul in bed. He puts his arm around her. She starts to calm down.

"No more sex tonight." She says.

Paul is disappointed, but doesn't argue.

"No more sex tonight." He repeats and kisses Laura on the forehead.

They lay in bed in silence and listen to the intermittent traffic outside. It's an eerie sort of calm now. The calm one feels after news of a family member passing away.

Helen had fallen asleep on the sofa while waiting for her daughter to come home. The front door clicks open and Helen awakens to see Laura in the doorway.

"Where were you? It's four in the morning for Christ's sake." Helen angrily.

"I was out and just lost track of time. It's Friday. I don't have school tomorrow."

"You forgot how to use a telephone and call? I'm sitting up all night worried where the hell my daughter is. I almost called the police."

"I'm sorry, I should have called." Laura said, moving past her mother to go upstairs. Laura's mind is elsewhere and not on her raving mother.

Helen blocks Laura from going upstairs.

"Were you with a boy?"

"I was not." Laura says feeling only a little guilty. Paul wasn't a boy, but a middle aged man. "I'm going to bed, mother." Helen steps aside.

"We will talk more about this in the morning." Helen says while hearing Laura shut and lock her bedroom door.

Helen is at a loss how to deal with her daughter. She also knows Laura is lying. She had smelled cologne on her.

Chapter 5

September, 1979

Angela wiped down the bar top after a quiet Sunday night at the Happy Hour—only forty dollars in tips tonight which is about half what Angela usually makes for a weekend. It's almost closing time, and the manager counts receipts while Angela gives the place a once-over. One final patron is still finishing his beer—late twenties, small and thin with stringy black hair and thick glasses.

"About time to go, Freddy." She says.

"I know, Angela." Freddy's tone is defeated.

"You ok?"

"Bar is empty. My bottle is almost empty. My bed is empty too." Freddy says, not making eye contact.

Angela has heard plenty of sob stories. Most stories contain the same checklist: dead-end jobs, cold wives, no wives, disrespectful kids, and unmet sexual desires. Angela had heard it all before, but Freddy was a little different. He was quieter and non-threatening. He never made sexual advances. She found him easy to talk to. There was also something a little unusual about Freddy Bile. He used to be an apprentice in a mortuary.

"Get yourself a girlfriend, Freddy. You're not going to find one in this dive."

"Why don't you be my girl, Angela? You're sweet. Let me guess, emotionally unavailable?" Freddy finally makes eye contact.

"You guessed it. Plus, I'm a mom. My attention is all on my little man at home." Angela says, tossing a dirty rag in the trash.

Freddy puts a twenty-dollar bill under his beer glass. He gets up from his barstool.

"I can't take a twenty, Freddy."

"You earned it tonight, angel face. See you tomorrow night." Freddy makes his way to the door and passes Tasha walking in. She walks to Angela and looks around the bar. Nobody is out front, so Tasha goes for a long kiss with Angela. They don't dare do that with people around. Their relationship was taboo and unbeknownst to anyone in town.

"Missed you, girl," Tasha says while looking into Angela's eyes.

"Missed you too."

"Was that the creepy mortician dude you were telling me about? Why is he here so late? Is he in love with you or something?" Tasha says, teasing.

"Ex-mortician. He's harmless."

"Better be. You're spoken for."

"Did you bring Billy?"

"He's fine. He's home. Patty is watching him. He ate."

"Always eating. Going to be a big boy." Angela says.

"He asks, 'where's momma.' Don't feel guilty. You're doing what you have to do." Tasha was trying to guard Angela's feelings.

"I'm never home. I miss the good times with him. Makes me sick."

"Gotta earn, love. When he's old enough, he will understand the sacrifice. He'll know his momma put him before anything else."

"Hope so."

"Now finish up so we can get home. You can watch him sleep. That counts." Tasha can see Angela getting teary-eyed. She wipes away a tear coming down her cheek.

At three in the morning, Freddy Bile sat inside his dark apartment. It wasn't much of anything. One television, one end table, and one lawn chair propped in front of the television. It was the cheapest place he could find in the southern end of town. Freddy sits in his chair in the dark. The television is off, and all Freddy has is his imagination. He thinks of Angela. Freddy always wanted a blonde woman. Ever since he saw Fay Wray in "King Kong," he fantasized about having one. When Freddy was a boy, he cut pictures out of catalogs of the prettiest ones. He would keep them under his mattress for alone and intimate times with himself.

Freddy's long-deceased mother had jet-black hair that went down to her waist. Freddy inherited her black hair, and he hated it. Kids would tease him and call him Dracula. Growing up, he never got attention from girls, especially the blonde ones that he pined for. He hated the kids at school, and he hated his mother too. Irene Dubois was a beatnik from California who migrated to New York City in 1955. She wanted to be an actress, but not the fluff she considered television and Hollywood films. She wanted serious work. She craved substance and an audience. Off-Broadway work was where she wanted to start. Being a single mother with a four-year-old son made it difficult to go on auditions. In reality, it wasn't even feasible. After a year of background and extra work, Irene was getting frustrated and getting close to being homeless. She moved herself and Freddy to Newark - close to the city but cheaper.

After a couple of years, Irene was around less and less. The television became Freddy's babysitter. Freddy loved it. Countless hours after school, if he went to school, were spent watching whatever was on. His favorites were old movies. The monster movies. "Frankenstein," "The Wolf Man," "Dracula," and "The Mummy" he memorized word for word. He spent hours doodling pictures of them in his schoolbooks. School and television are all Freddy had. Few friends, no father figures, and no church services to attend.

Irene would stumble in from time to time with a new man or woman she had met. She would put some food in the refrigerator for Freddy. Milk and lunch meat mostly. If Irene did stay at the two-bedroom apartment, she would mostly smoke marijuana with whoever she had brought home. Irene and her friend or friends would have bizarre conversations. Freddy could pick out keywords while sitting in front of the television. "Rabbits," "altar," "purity," "court," and "feast" were just some of the words he remembered. Freddy never asked his mother about where she had disappeared to. He didn't really care, and she never cared to tell him.

There was never guidance or nurturing, let alone love, between Freddy and his mother. Irene treated Freddy like a pet. A pet she didn't want. With the lack of a structured home life, Freddy had flunked out of school by thirteen. It was during this pubescent period that Freddy got more acquainted with his mother's friends. They were an eclectic group of miscreants and misfits. Young, old, addicts, hippies, perverts, transients and whatever else passed through Newark on their way to New York City. Sometimes Irene would throw parties, and Freddy would talk to whoever he found the least intimidating.

One man in particular interested Freddy. His mother had referred to him as an "elder." Freddy didn't quite understand the moniker. The man wasn't much older than his mother. His name was Shawn Billes. Freddy liked Shawn since he never had older male role models and never talked to any older men before he met Shawn. Freddy would eventually change his last name from Dubois to Bile as a tribute to Shawn Billes. Shawn identified himself as a sanguinarian. Freddy assumed it was a religious group like Catholic, Baptist, or a nationality.

"No, it's a lifestyle, Frederick. I need to for health reasons. It's like being a vegetarian, but instead of vegetables, I drink blood." Shawn told Freddy. Freddy was now very curious.

"A vampire?"

"No, it's for my digestion. I can't process regular food. I can get sick." Shawn was tall and wiry. Some teeth were missing. Freddy thought he didn't look healthy.

"Human blood?" Freddy asks.

"Willing human donors. Your mother is a donor. That's how we met. She supplies some of us with blood once a month. She is a dear woman. We all love Irene." Shawn says, watching Irene by the window smoking grass with another woman in sunglasses.

"Do you bite her neck?"

"No, she cuts herself. Not deep, just tiny cuts we can drink from."

"What does it taste like?" Freddy asks with caution.

"You never bit the inside of your cheek? Bit your own tongue? Blood tastes like blood. Metallic. It varies on a person's diet." Shawn tells Freddy while rolling a joint.

After a half dozen more visits and hundreds of questions for Shawn and her mother's friends, Freddy began to piece together where his mother was going and what she was doing. The reference to rabbits was for them being used in blood rituals. Her odd hours were sanguinarian hours, as she had to be at their beck and call. The reference to an altar was literally an altar where she would be nude and make tiny cuts on her body for them to feed from. She wanted to become the one and only blood donor for her group. They all treated her as special because her blood was the purest. Irene was not a virgin, but she carried no disease.

"It's important to belong to a greater cause, Freddy." Irene would tell her son.

Now Freddy Bile sat in his apartment at the age of twenty-eight and recollected his mother and her death. She died alone twelve years prior in a hospital in Newark. Freddy had visited once. Irene Dubois had contracted hepatitis. Her liver failed, and her death was quite painful. Fluid had filled her brain cavity, causing hallucinations and seizures. Before falling ill, she did performance art in underground fetish clubs in the city. Bloodletting demonstrations with sanguinarians and the mentally ill who fancied themselves living vampires. The only fame she ever achieved was in these closeted vampire communities. Freddy hated her. Even the day he found out she died after suffering seven consecutive seizures. Freddy now thought of Angela. Blonde hair, blue eyes, fair skin, and a sweet smile. He had memorized every conversation they had. He knew she had a son named Billy. He knew she was poor and living with that black woman. He knew he had to have her and would stop at nothing to get her.

Chapter 6

Late September, 1979

Laura sat on the edge of her bed, a nervous wreck. Between biting her fingernails and tapping her left foot on the wood floor, she would stare at the telephone on her night table. She told the gynecologist that she would be home between two and five in the afternoon. One phone call could change her life forever. It was a phone call she had been dreading.

All ties with Paul were cut. There was too much to do and too much to see still. Laura had wanted to graduate, see the world a little bit and then get a career. She did not want to be saddled with a baby at seventeen. Laura told Paul to stop dropping by the grocery store and to stop following her home after school. Two days ago, it had escalated into a yelling match behind the grocery. The argument was so bad that Laura assumed the relationship was over. She has not seen or heard from Paul since.

A month has passed since their first and last sexual encounter. Cramps and nausea started two weeks ago. Laura had put off taking a pregnancy test. She didn't trust them. She wanted a professional opinion. The opinion was on the other side of the telephone she stared at. Laura had hoped and prayed she wasn't pregnant. She prayed even though her family wasn't religious. Her mother didn't believe in organized religion, and her father could take it or leave it. When he was alive. If her mother found out she was pregnant, she could only imagine the hell that would be brought down on her. She assumed she would be kicked out of the house.

The phone rang. After all the waiting, one would think Laura would snatch up the receiver. She didn't. She let it ring three times before picking it up.

"Hello. Yes, this is she." A pained look started to come over her face. "We can talk about that…..I see….. Thank you very much…..I can start regular appointments next month…..My mother's insurance should cover it…..Goodbye." Laura hangs up the phone, and tears begin streaming down her cheeks. Laura is a pregnant teenager.

Across town is Paul's garage. He is changing a serpentine belt on a Mitsubishi Galant.

"Foreign piece of crap," Paul says through gritted teeth as he pulls the wrench to loosen the belt from the gears.

After removing the belt, he wipes his forehead with a greasy shop towel. Paul isn't frustrated with the foreign car, the belt, or even the lack of business. He is upset with Laura. He hasn't spoken to her in two days.

"There are worse things in the world than being with me, babe." He told her during their last talk. Fight.

"You think you can do better than me? Fat chance. Who else will take care of you? You're my girl." He said.

Paul could not figure out why Laura had left. He had gone over every word she told him repeatedly in his mind. It was eating a hole in his stomach. This was the first time in Paul's life he had been denied something he wanted. He wanted Laura, and he wanted a family with her. She was making that difficult. Paul thought perhaps she was seeing someone else, but he must have been doing a good job of eluding Paul's surveillance of Laura. Paul had parked his truck down the street from Laura's house the past two nights. Her routine had not changed. Perhaps it was Helen who was keeping them apart. The thoughts never stopped, and not knowing was driving Paul crazy.

Paul stood by his workbench and closed his eyes. He thought about a conversation they had one week ago outside her high school along the gated fence that enclosed the football field. He had cornered her.

"We might be a family. What's wrong with that? Move in with me. Is that what you want?"

"I don't want any of this. This is too much, Paul. I'm not ready." Laura says, feeling trapped.

"Have you told your mother?"

"No. Of course not. I'm not even sure yet. If I am pregnant, I should have it taken care of." Laura said, looking away from Paul's stare.

"Taken care of? You mean get rid of it? Abortion?" Paul says, feeling his temperature rising.

"It's an option."

"That is not an option. You are not killing my child." Paul is inches from Laura's face. She turns her cheek to him and looks down at the ground. She becomes fixated on a dandelion growing through a crack in the sidewalk. She is mesmerized by the beauty and simplicity of it.

"Get that thought out of your head, Laura." Paul reaches his hand up onto Laura's neck. He wants to make her look at him and make her understand because he doesn't have the words. He would never physically harm Laura. His hand comes down, and he turns away and walks to his truck.

"One day, you'll see, Laura. One day we'll be together. A family." Paul gets in his truck and drives off.

Laura has not taken her teary and swollen eyes off the dandelion. She wants to be it.

Alone and thriving and beautiful. She then remembers a dandelion is not a flower but a weed.

Another week had passed between Paul and Laura with no talk. This morning Laura had parked by a nondescript numbered medical office. Laura is sitting in her car, twirling her hair. Her eyes are a million miles away. Building seven is family dentistry, building eight is a podiatrist, and building nine is SMITH'S COUNSELING FOR WOMEN. Laura knows of building nine from her mother. Helen would tell Laura about the poor and unfortunate girls that would visit the emergency room at the hospital and then be referred to building nine. It was the practice of Dr. Charles Smith. He offered counseling to rape victims, abused women, and teenage girls wanting abortions. The word abortion was never mentioned in the hospital or inside building nine. Abortions were called "procedures."

Laura watched a tall thin, older man with wispy gray hair exit his car. She assumed this was the doctor. He looked like a ghost. His head was down, his gait was long, and he entered building nine. Laura imagines what the procedure would be like. First, filling out paperwork, changed clothes, and sat alone in a sterile, cold room. Dr. Smith walked in and made light pleasantries and then was wheeled into some surgical room. The procedure she couldn't imagine. She wasn't sure if you were anesthetized or just numbed up. Laura would overhear other girls' conversations at school. Some of the more popular girls had gotten abortions. She had heard stories of long vacuum tubes being inserted and having the unborn evacuated. She worried if it was painful. One girl at school said she had severe cramps and bleeding. Laura couldn't believe she had gotten herself into this. Her first sexual encounter, and this is the price she had to pay. She cursed Paul and herself. She started to sweat and feel overwhelmed. Laura closed her eyes to relax but started feeling nauseous in the car. She decided to drive home instead of entering building nine.

Laura lays on her bed, and the quiet stillness of the day was bittersweet. The mid morning sun has pierced through the partially open curtains. The shafts of sunlight showed the floating dust in the room. Laura had thought of Paul and his wanting to be a family. Laura lay on her side of the bed and watched the sunlight on her carpeted floor. The warmth in the room made Laura think of warm things. Babies are warm. Dr. Smith's office is cold, she imagined. His long, old, gray, thin fingers would be cold too. Laura dozed on and off. When it was two in the afternoon, she awakened, and her first thought was of having Paul's baby.

Chapter 7

October, 1979

Paul's truck is overflowing with Laura's belongings. It is parked in front of her house. Her former house. Paul is carrying some bundled-up bed clothes, and Laura is right behind him with her record albums tucked under her left arm. Laura only glances back at the only home she has ever known. Helen is peeking through the living room curtains, watching her daughter leave. Paul and Laura get in the truck. Paul puts his hand on Laura's shoulder. Her eyes are swollen from crying.

"She'll come around," Paul says.

"Just drive."

The truck pulls away. Helen watches, closes the curtains and sits on the living room sofa. She looks to her right and sees family pictures framed on the mantle over the fireplace. She stared at a black and white photo of Laura when she was a baby. Helen remembers the day the photo was taken. Seventeen years ago seems like yesterday. The revelation of the pregnancy and the ensuing argument were quick and devastating. Laura would not consider abortion, and Helen refused to help with the child when it was born. Helen worked all the time and knew she would do most of the child-rearing as Laura went to school. She knew Paul and his type. One diaper change, and he would have nothing more to do with that child. He was a drunk and spent most of his free time downtown drinking. Paul was not a provider, and her daughter was too young to be a mother. Helen also knew that the baby would not be raised properly.

Helen now sits in her house. It feels like a house and not a home anymore. Alone and quiet. Too quiet. The creaking of old wood as the sun beats on the side of the house in autumn. Helen walks to the kitchen, looks out the back window into the yard, and sees the rusty old swing set. She remembers Laura's father pushing her on it. Higher and higher, she would go laughing all the while. Memories of a broken family and the quiet, creaking house are all that is left for Helen Krueger.

Paul and Laura sit in the truck in Paul's driveway. Laura is in a fog as she stares out the passenger window. A month ago, her life was normal. Now her life is upside down. She feels guilty and also blames Paul.

Paul is doing his best to conceal his joy. A young, pregnant woman of his very own. A family of his very own. Paul is selfish but not completely oblivious. He knows Laura is upset, so he does his best to match her mood.

"We should go inside." He says, exiting the truck.

Laura sits in the car for a few more moments and ruminates on her feelings. It wasn't her mother's anger that bothered her. It was a disappointment. Her mother had never been disappointed in her before, and this feeling was something that she couldn't compartmentalize. It hurt her heart. Laura entertained thoughts of just running away and leaving it behind, but there was nowhere to go. Acting on impulse had gotten her into this.

Paul is unloading the truck bed. He glances up to see Laura still in the passenger seat. Paul knew this wouldn't be easy, but he was grateful that she had stopped crying.

The first few weeks of living together were good. The two had settled into a routine. Paul was at work during the day while Laura was entering her senior year of high school. She was determined to finish no matter what. She wasn't showing noticeably yet, but that would change soon enough. At night the two had dinner together. Laura would get home from the grocery store

at seven, so dinner was usually around eight. She was determined to keep working as well. After

dinner, Paul would watch television, and Laura would do homework and read her pile of baby

books. The spare bedroom in the house filled with mementos from Paul's childhood was gone,

and the room was now a nursery. Everything seemed normal, as normal can be with a

forty-seven-year-old man living with his pregnant seventeen-year-old girlfriend. Something was

amiss. Laura was feeling isolated.

Laura hadn't spoken to her mother since she left, and the few friends Laura did have, she

didn't have much time to see or socialize with. Even less than she had before, which was little.

The previous Saturday, she had made plans with a girl from work to buy baby clothes, but her car

would not start, and she had to cancel. On Sundays, Laura would go to the local Toms River flea

market on Route 70, but last Sunday, Paul had complained of a cough, and with the late autumn

chill, Laura didn't want to leave him sick and alone at home. Laura began to feel that she was

blending into the house, like the faded brown and yellow wallpaper. Disappearing.

Paul was never happier. He would watch Laura decorate the nursery with furniture, paint,

and new toys for a boy or a girl. Paul felt more and more like a father as time passed and the

leaves turned from yellow to orange. Neither had wanted to know the sex of the baby yet. Paul

wanted a son. Laura secretly hoped for a girl.

One day at work, Paul began to feel guilty. He looked down at the counter at his cheese

and lettuce sandwich. Next to it were two spark plugs. Paul felt bad for disconnecting Laura's car

battery a couple of weeks ago when she wanted to go shopping for baby clothes. He felt bad for

faking illness and keeping her home. Paul thought a pregnant woman should always be home and

not go around town. She should not be risking her son's life. Paul needs a son to feel like a man -

virile, potent, and able. After his father, Jack, died, Paul wanted the Phy name to carry on. There was no other lineage in the family. Now, looking down at the two spark plugs he took out of Laura's engine, he changed his mind. Paul would put them back in tonight so she could go shopping for his future son this weekend.

Chapter 8

November, 1979

Freddy sat at the back of the Happy Hour bar watching the New Jersey Devils game. He was half watching the game and half watching Angela at the front of the bar deflect advances from the patrons. Occasionally she would laugh with a co-worker or a customer. Her laugh filled the room, and it was just another little thing about Angela that Freddy found irresistible. Freddy was feeling pensive. Tonight he wanted to be a little bold with her. He wasn't sure if a joke would do or if just throwing her a compliment that she had probably heard a thousand times was the way to go. Freddy had gotten carried away with his imagination when he was alone in his apartment. He had imagined dating Angela, becoming boyfriend and girlfriend, making love, getting married, and having a baby. Hours would pass until the realization hit that he was alone. That's when the depression would come.

Angela notices Freddy sitting alone and starts to walk over. His heart skips a beat.

"Why are you sitting here alone?" She asks.

"Just watching the game. I haven't finished this beer yet, so I don't dare to flirt with you." Freddy tried jokingly.

"Thanksgiving is coming up. Any plans with your family?" Angela asks curiously, not knowing if Freddy even has a family.

"Nah, family is gone. My mother passed away some time ago."

"You never talk about your mother. Why is that? If I'm being too nosy, just tap me on the nose." Angela says with a smile.

"Not much to tell. She wasn't much of a mother. I have no complaints, though. I'm here sitting in a bar with a girl with the face of an angel, so things didn't turn out too bad."

"You're too sweet, Freddy Bile."

"What are you doing for Thanksgiving, angel face?" Freddy asks.

"Just me and my son."

"Billy, right?"

"Yep. The apple of my eye. Eighteen months old." Angela says proudly.

"Do you have help with him? It's just you?"

"Friends babysit when they can. Most of my family, what's left of them, are in Pennsylvania." Angela says. Her heart hurts a little saying this, as she has not seen any of her family since she got pregnant.

Angela had a typical middle-class suburban upbringing. Her father worked in the dying steel industry, and her mother was a homemaker. She had a younger brother who died of crib death at one time. It would later be called SIDS. Angela had always gotten the attention of boys growing up and had her fair share of boyfriends in high school. Angela wanted to fall in love with a boy but could never find the right one. She had slept around. Looking for that spark, the fireworks a girl is supposed to get when she meets the one. It never happened. All that happened was an unwanted pregnancy. Since Angela had slept with at least half a dozen boys in her high school, she had no idea who the father was. She was ashamed and petrified of what her parents would think. The fear was too much when she started to show in the second trimester. Angela ran away from home at eighteen. She got as far as a Philadelphia bus station, where she met Roy "Priest" Higgins. He was polite and kind to Angela and offered her money to come with him. He promised he could find her work even if she was pregnant. Angela was desperate, scared, alone, and needed a place to stay. Roy was true to his word and got Angela a job at the gentleman's club as a bookkeeper. He saw the potential in her after that baby was out. Angela settled into an apartment Priest had gotten her. It was her second week on the job that Angela finally saw fireworks. She had made eye contact with a black dancer with striking features and hazel green eyes. She had seen Tasha Higgins.

"What about the boy's father?" Freddy asks.

"He's not around," Angela says.

A big meaty hand lands on Freddy's shoulder. Paul sits down already with a beer in hand.

"Talking to my girl, Freddy?" Paul says, buzzing.

"Hey, Paulie, we're just talking about Angela's boy. Did you tell Angela about your baby?"

"Get out! You're having a baby, Paul?" Angela asks.

"Yeah, Laura and I are just thrilled about it. She is practically glowing."

"Sex?" Angela wonders.

"Not for a month. Kind of a personal question." Paul gives Angela a shifty glance.

"Not you, the baby. The sex of the baby."

"Oh, we want it to be a surprise. I want a boy. It'll be a boy. Laura wants a girl. What about you, Freddy? What's new with you?" Paul shifts the conversation.

"Four burials today. Flu season. Nature's way of cleaning house." Freddy says with a smirk.

Angela pours another round for Paul and Freddy.

"Drink up, boys."

She moves to the main bar and changes the jukebox to "Marie's the Name" by Elvis Presley. Angela's middle name is Marie. While by the jukebox, Paul checks out her backside.

"That girl was built to sin, Freddy. Shame she's a dike."

Freddy's eyes widen, and he puts down his beer.

"Why do you say that?" He asks.

"Ever notice the black chick that comes in just before closing?" Paul asks.

Freddy nods yes, his mind jumbled at this theory Paul has.

"There you go. Two women can't stand to be out of each other's sight for more than a day. They also live together. Come on, Freddy." Paul says, swigging down his beer. It dribbles out of the corners of his mouth.

"I know they live together. They're friends."

"Sure, Freddy, just friends."

Paul begins to tell Freddy about one night not long ago. Before Paul found out about Laura's pregnancy, he had toyed with the idea of being with Angela. He was also drunk. Paul, doing what he does best, decided to follow Angela home one night after closing time. He parked across from the trailer park she lived in and just walked through as casually as he could. It was a poorly lit park, so Paul could easily camouflage himself against the bushes and the window looking into the living room portion of the mobile home. He watched them eat a very late dinner together, holding hands. He then watched the two move over to the sofa after dinner and begin kissing. He could see naked bodies between the cheap curtains that hung over the window. For the first fifteen minutes, Paul was in shock. He was aroused for the last fifteen minutes and masturbated in the bushes. After finishing, Paul slunk back to his truck across the street and left.

"Damn lucky you weren't caught," Freddy says.

"It was worth it. Sorry, Freddy, they're dikes."

Freddy is unable to process all this. Moments ago, he was in love with a young woman. Now that dream is shattering. He was pining away for someone who would never be interested in him. Perhaps Paul was embellishing or making up lies to have Angela to himself. Freddy couldn't decide which. Perhaps Paul witnessed a one-time thing brought on by loneliness or alcohol. Angela turning down advances from the men at the bar, began to make sense. Maybe Paul was telling the truth. Freddy had to find out for himself.

As the Happy Hour closes for the night, Freddy is across the parking lot, hiding behind a tree. He waits in the cold late autumn night for the door to open and for Angela and Tasha to come out. To kill time and keep the blood flowing, he stomps his feet in the dirt and blows them into his hands. When he sees headlights from a passing car, he crouches down. He is hidden, but the beams from a passing car could spoil his cover. A police car is coming down Water Street, and Freddy watches it from his perch. He can see a black, husky officer behind the wheel. Freddy knows Officer Clarence Gardener through the cemetery. If a cop was killed in the line of duty or if a retired police officer passed away, then Officer Gardener would be leading the procession of dozens of police cruisers through the cemetery.

Freddy is starting to get nervous as Officer Gardener makes a second pass in front of the Happy Hour, but the cruiser continues down Water Street and makes a right onto Main Street. Now, under cover of darkness and the police presence is gone, Freddy relaxes a bit. The door opens, and out comes Angela and Tasha. He watches as Angela locks the door and walks with Tasha to the only car in the parking lot, a green Chevelle. Tasha gets in the driver's seat, and Angela gets in the passenger seat. The car rumbles but sits. The hot exhaust from the tailpipe mixes with the cool air causing steam. Freddy emerges from his hiding place and starts to creep toward the Chevelle. He stays low and approaches from behind. Ten feet behind the Chevelle, Freddy takes cover behind a garbage can in the center of the lot. He can barely see into the fogging rear window. Freddy's heart sinks as he sees Angela and Tasha in a deep, passionate kiss. All he can feel is a rush of blood to his head, and nausea sets in. He turns and slinks away into the night with the knowledge that Paul is telling him the truth.

In his apartment, Freddy sits in his lawn chair facing the television. The television is off, and he stares at his silhouette on the screen. Tonight he wanted to flirt a little with Angela, make a move, and get to know her a little more. He got to know a whole lot more than he had bargained for. Tasha was the object of her affection, leaving Freddy feeling even more alone. Most people would just move on and look for someone else, but Freddy was fixated on Angela. He had never felt this way about a woman before, and it took a lifetime, in his mind, to find her. He simply could not give up. He knew there must be a way to drive a wedge between Angela and Tasha. It would be tough. He didn't know Tasha, so poking holes in her character was impossible. Then it struck like a thunderbolt.

"The boy," Freddy says to himself.

Freddy's plan was simple. Play on Angela's insecurity about raising her son without a male influence. Freddy began to draw his plans to bring Angela to him. He would use the boy's need for a father figure to give him an in with Angela and hopefully push Tasha on the outs.

Tasha's love for Billy was endless. No children of her own left plenty of room in her heart for Billy. She had fantasized about having a large family when she was a little girl. Six in all is what she wanted. To get that, she needed a husband. That's where things got complicated. She could never see herself being a wife. The husband, she would imagine, was nameless and faceless. There was no emotional attachment to the husband in her fantasized family. To Tasha, it was about the children. The man was insignificant.

While Angela is at the Happy Hour, Tasha watches Billy sleep in his crib. Her mind drifted off to the previous night, kissing Angela in the car after work. Her mind then drifts off into the future. Her and Angela watching Billy playing in the sand at the beach. Billy is a teenager, and her teaching him how to drive. Giving him advice on girls he liked. The thoughts weren't realistic. To be in an open relationship with a woman without stares or snide remarks wasn't possible. Angela had been very cautious about public affection. Tasha would never force Angela out for fear of pushing her away in the process. A closeted love affair, it would stay for the foreseeable future.

Billy rolled over on his stomach. Tasha quickly nudged him to his side. Angela had told Tasha about her brother, who died from crib death. Tasha had read that some infants aren't strong enough to breathe on their own when lying on their stomachs. She had a genuine and caring nature, which Angela had found attractive in Tasha. Tasha had found Angela's innocence the most attractive aspect of her. Together they were a team. Tasha glanced at the clock on the wall and thought of her other baby, who would be home soon from work.

Slow night at the Happy Hour, and Angela is by the jukebox going through the selections. She punches in "Lonely Boy" by Andrew Gold. Over her left shoulder at the far end of the bar and watching her is Freddy. Angela feels a stare and turns and catches him. Freddy doesn't avert his eyes. He just smiles. Angela walks over to him.

"Slow tonight, Freddy. Give me a big tip so I can eat this week." Angela says, leaning on the bar next to him.

"I always leave you a tip, but I do have to get home soon. Work at seven a.m. I don't sleep much anymore. I nap during the day."

"Like a vampire."

"Like a vampire," Freddy says with a smile.

"I have to get home to my little man."

"Who watches Billy? Is it that friend you were telling me about? Tasha?"

"Yeah, she does most of the work. I feel terrible about that." Angela says, looking down a little ashamed.

"Father not in the picture at all?"

"No, just me and my son."

"No other family? Siblings?" Freddy asks. Probing.

"Estranged. I did have a brother. He died at three months old." Angela is wiping down the bar.

"It was just my mother and I growing up. Never met my father. My mother was an actress."

"An actress? In anything I've seen?" Angela asks.

"No. Off-Broadway stuff. I would have liked to have known my father. Maybe my mother would have been a nicer person. I remember being jealous of other kids and their fathers. Catch in the park, learning to ride a bicycle. Things like that. I sometimes think my life would have turned out differently if I had known him." Freddy says while looking up at Angela, who seems to be staring into space. "Darkness on the Edge of Town" by Bruce Springsteen begins to play on the jukebox.

Freddy's words hit Angela in her heart. She also worries that a lack of a male influence in Billy's life could be a problem. She needed someone eventually to show him how to be a man. She couldn't do that, and neither could Tasha. They can provide a home and love but not the necessary tools a growing boy needs to become a self-sufficient man. Angela had to push those concerns aside for a later date and just try to keep a roof over everyone's heads. The stress of that had caused her to question her path. She often thought of her family back home in Pennsylvania. Sometimes she wished she could go back.

"It's getting late, Freddy. Closing in a few." Angela says distantly.

"You're right, angel face. I should get going." Freddy stands, but not before leaving a ten-dollar bill under his glass.

"Good night, Freddy." Angela doesn't notice Freddy leaving. She is still in a half-trance. She scans the Happy Hour and sees a couple of old men getting up to leave. They remind her of her father. Billy would need a father, and Angela didn't know where to find him. What Angela knew was that Tasha couldn't do that. Doubt began to creep in. Doubt about her choices and about Tasha.

Freddy's plan began to work.

Chapter 9

December, 1979

The pain was extraordinary. Laura grabs her stomach and leans over the bathroom sink. The fifth month of her pregnancy has been the hardest by far. Morning sickness, intermittent bouts of nausea, sleepless nights and now sharp pains in her abdomen. The doctor had told Laura that in the fourth and fifth months, the baby's weight would double, and it did. Laura's belly popped out so far so fast that her abdominal muscles ached under the strain. Her belly wasn't ready, and neither was Laura. The pain started to dull, so Laura took a seat on the toilet and breathed. Constipation and heartburn were other tiny side effects that paled in comparison to her other symptoms. Doubts were creeping into Laura's mind. She felt this was the universe's way of saying she should have aborted the pregnancy. Twelve to fifteen more weeks of this suffering would feel like an eternity.

To distract herself from the pain, Laura often thought of baby names. For a girl, she liked Michelle, Melissa, or April after the possible birth month. As a boy, Paul liked Paul Junior, Evan, or Michael. Laura had been pining away for a girl and had already started to buy pink baby clothes in secret. These were the nice distractions Laura enjoyed in an otherwise dreadful experience.

Doctor Pam O'Brien was Laura's OBGYN at Community Hospital in Toms River. Laura trusted her implicitly and even looked at her as a motherly figure considering Laura's real mother had very little to do with her anymore. Dr. O'Brien was in her early sixties, which comforted

Laura greatly, as did the half dozen degrees on her office walls. Laura thought of making an appointment today to see her, especially now that Laura saw her bleeding gums in the bathroom mirror, but her car would not start.

Paul sat at the front counter of his garage. Customers trickled in, but business was poor. Oil changes and tire patches. Not much money. In his downtime, Paul contemplated his new family and his future. He wanted a boy and imagined him playing football, dating girls, driving, getting married, and taking over the family business if there was anything left of it. In Paul's fantasies, Laura would be right by his side, happy and looking at him lovingly. The happy Phy family sounded better than the quiet Phy family he had heard growing up. After Paul's son was an adult, the fantasy stopped. Paul couldn't imagine himself as a man in his seventies or eighties. To be feeble and weak was too scary a thought for Paul. He wanted to be a young man again, and maybe through his son, he could be. He could be popular, smart, attractive and full of hope. To Paul, it would be like getting a second chance. A chance to make things right or at least better than what they had turned out to be.

Laura's pain in her stomach had bothered Paul. He knew she wanted to see this doctor she raved about, but Paul couldn't take the chance of his pregnant girlfriend driving around town in pain. If she had gotten distracted while driving and something had happened, Paul would never forgive himself. That's why he disconnected her car battery earlier in the morning.

The following day, Paul sat in the waiting room of Dr. O'Brien's office and was flipping through a fishing magazine. Inside the exam room, Laura was lying down on her back in a gown while Dr. O'Brien massaged along the sides of Laura's swollen belly.

"Nothing unusual. Your muscles are stretching, that's all. I would suggest some exercises to strengthen the area." Dr. O'Brien says while pulling the gown down over Laura's stomach.

"Thank God. I just got worried." Laura says while looking into her doctor's sympathetic eyes.

"Is there anyone besides your partner that you can talk to?"

"Paul is very excited about the baby. He's all I need. We're getting married after things settle a bit. Anyone else? I haven't talked to my mother in months."

A little silence passes between the doctor and the patient as a click is heard. The heat kicks on, and at that moment, Dr. O'Brien knows Laura is feeling alone and scared.

"Things change. Every mother wants to see her grandchildren."

"I hope so. It does get lonely sometimes. Especially at night when I can't sleep. I walk around the house and just think."

"Think about what?" The doctor asks.

"Choices. I'm not sure I've made very good choices. I dropped out last week and will just get the general equivalency. The kids at school have noticed that I'm pregnant. It just got to be too much." Laura says, teary-eyed.

"I want you to see me anytime you're feeling overwhelmed. It's good to talk about things that are going on in your life. I'm here to help you, Laura. In more ways than one."

Dr. Pam O'Brien worried about Laura and the possible depression she could slip into. Postpartum depression was a possibility too. Dr. O'Brien worried, as much as a doctor will allow themselves to worry, and thought that just having Laura talk about her problems would be a good start. In her gut, the doctor knew Laura was not ready to be a mother. *Because you can have a baby doesn't mean you should have a baby.* Dr. O'Brien had seen many unfortunate cases in her past. Suicides, child abuse, neglect, abandonment, and even infanticide were not unheard of among teenage mothers. She could never let on to Laura Krueger that she worried for her.

Putting that thought into her head could scare her even more. The best approach was to listen and hope that Laura would not become just another unfortunate statistic.

"White Christmas" by Bing Crosby plays while Angela serves drinks to Paul and Freddy. The Christmas tree in the Happy Hour shows like a pink star in the corner of the room. It was seven feet tall and stood by the stage where local bands occasionally performed.

"Laura is doing better. Certain exercises should take care of the pain. She was worried. I wasn't." Paul tells Freddy.

"That's good to hear, Paul," Freddy says while watching Angela come over with a pitcher of beer.

"How are you, Angie? Keeping Freddy in line? He doesn't look much, but he's a real troublemaker." Paul says with a smile.

"Don't have to tell me twice," Angela says with a wink to Freddy as she serves another customer.

"How are things going with you two?" Paul asks.

"We had Thanksgiving together, well, the day after Thanksgiving. Took her to an Italian place on Fisher Boulevard. Was nice. We just talked."

"She's still a dike, Freddy. Don't want you getting your hopes up." A sympathetic Paul was rare.

"I know, but it was good. I even met her son. He's almost two. Beautiful boy. She took him to the restaurant." Freddy says, with a touch of arrogance.

"That's a pretty big deal. She must like you if she lets you meet her kid. That's a big step for a woman. So I've heard. What about her girlfriend, Tasha?"

"I haven't met her. Maybe Angela is bisexual. She obviously has been with men."

"I suppose anything is possible. Did you find out anything about the father of her kid?"

"She changed the subject. Probably the abusive, controlling type." Freddy says.

"I like him already." Paul laughs.

Freddy gets up to use the bathroom but is intercepted by Angela, who grabs his shoulders from behind. She pulls him back a couple of feet.

"What are we doing, angel?" Freddy was surprised at the touching.

"Look up, dummy."

Freddy does and sees a mistletoe. He becomes flush as Angela gives him a quick peck on the lips.

"Merry Christmas, Mr. Bile."

"Merry Christmas, Ms. Mallek."

Paul was watching from his barstool.

"Shit, maybe she is bi," Paul says under his breath.

Inside the bathroom, Freddy is washing his hands. He looks up into the mirror and can see the faint whisper of red lipstick of Angela's on his mouth. He tastes it with his tongue.

Light snow falls outside the trailer window. Inside, Tasha sits in the warm glow of the two-foot-tall Christmas tree in the living room. She has a glass of cranberry vodka and is in her bathrobe. Tonight she will not be driving Angela home. Angela's new friend, Freddy, will be doing that. When Angela is home, she seems distant. She doesn't share every detail of her day with Tasha like she used to. It all started to change when Freddy crept into their lives. The first warning sign was the day after Thanksgiving when he took Angela and Billy to dinner and the tree lighting downtown. Tasha gets up and checks on Billy in his crib to distract herself from these moments. Soon he will be too big for the crib, and he will get his own bed. He's out like a light, and Tasha pulls the covers up.

Tasha quietly checks under the Christmas tree in the living room and sees the dozens of gifts for Billy this year. It was mostly clothing and stuffed animals. One gift seems out of place. It was a big stuffed doll of "The Count" from "Sesame Street." Tasha immediately knew it was from Freddy. She checked the gift tag, and sure enough, she was correct. "To William From Frederick."

Another hour passes, and Angela quietly walks in from the cold. Tasha is smoking a cigarette on the end of the couch.

"Hey, babe," Angela whispers so as not to wake Billy.

"Hey, yourself."

"Billy eat?"

"He did. I'm guessing Frederick drove you home?" Tasha had a slight tinge of annoyance in her voice.

"Frederick? Freddy, yes, he did." Angela sits on the couch on the opposite end.

"You know that fool is in love with you."

"Aren't all men? He's not, and even if he is, it doesn't matter because I'm spoken for." Angela says, looking at Tasha, who is looking only at the Christmas tree.

"He's going to try and break us up. Taking you out and buying you and the baby things. He wants to be Billy's father, and we both know he isn't. Does he even know that we're together, or does he think we're just friends?" Tasha says.

"He probably suspects, but I'm not sure why we are even talking about him. He's just a friend. Freddy is just a lonely guy."

"Lonely men are dangerous. You're leading a dangerous man on, which is why I'm upset

with you. He gives you things, and that hurts me because I give you things. You don't need him."
Tasha puts her cigarette out in the ashtray sitting on the arm of the couch.

"No, I don't need him. I need you. I need you to be happy. I need Billy to be happy."
Angela watches Tasha leave the room without even a look.

Sitting alone in silence in the soft glow of the Christmas tree, Angela starts to think of ways to fix things with Tasha. She loves her and finds it difficult to imagine a life without her. Perhaps taking her to dinner and lovemaking after would smooth things over. She thinks being single would make things easier, *but who would care for the baby*? Her mind wanders, and she begins to think of Billy. She doesn't want Billy clinging to her his whole life. He needs to learn to be independent, strong and capable. Billy needs a father figure. Angela needed to make some choices, and they may be very tough ones. At that moment, Billy wakes up and begins to cry.

Freddy is taking a dimly lit back road home. While driving, he thinks about how wonderful the past few weeks have been. Getting closer to Angela and meeting her son Billy, or William as Freddy likes to call him, had been better than he had imagined. He felt a sense of purpose for the first time in a long time. He felt responsible for Angela and Williams's well-being. To be a father is the most important job a man can have, and Freddy was hopeful to be at least a stepfather. He just needed Tasha out of the picture. Freddy can do that without ever having to speak with her. Angela would do the work for him. All he had to do was plant seeds of doubt and advantageously position himself. Make himself a stable alternative to the current home life Angela has now.

Up ahead on the dimly lit road is a clump of fur with a trail of blood behind it. It was barely noticeable with the light snow covering it, but Freddy had a keen eye. Someone had recently run over what looked to be a raccoon. The black stripes on the tail give it away. Freddy pulls up next to it. No other cars are around him tonight. He gets out, walks around his car, and opens the trunk. Inside, it is lined with plastic bags, and a shovel is in the middle. Freddy takes the shovel and walks to the raccoon to inspect it. In one scoop, he takes the bloodied carcass of the animal and dumps it into his plastic-lined trunk. He leaves the shovel next to the raccoon and closes the trunk. Sitting in the driver's seat, he thinks about preparing the animal for consumption. He will not be eating it. He will be drinking from it.

Chapter 10

April, 1980

Laura is staring out the window of her hospital room. A saline drip pumping into a vein in her left hand. Saline is provided to patients to prevent dehydration which Laura has been suffering from. Paul is asleep in a chair next to Laura's hospital bed. Last night the pain was intense after Laura's water broke. In a panic, Paul rushed her to the hospital, but as soon as they arrived, the pain had subsided. The shot of morphine helped. Contractions are now thirty minutes apart, and Dr. O'Brien is on her way. In the few quiet moments Laura has left, she refuses to dwell on the past and instead tries to focus on the future. Paul had been more attentive recently; even her mother had called to talk with her. She still felt alone, just not as alone.

Dr. Pam O'Brien enters in full scrubs, and Paul wakes up. She sits at the foot of the hospital bed.

"How are you feeling, Laura?" O'Brien asks while lifting up the sheet.

"Uncomfortable."

"The morphine takes time to kick in. Bend your knees." Dr. O'Brien's gloved right-hand feels around the cervix. Five centimeters dilated.

"I haven't felt the baby move in an hour."

Dr. O'Brien's eyes widened. There is a flurry of activity by nurses, and the bed is moved to the delivery room. It all happens so fast that Laura and Paul don't know what's happening. Paul is asked to wait in the room as Laura is whisked away. He hopes this means she's ready to give birth, but he knows something is wrong.

"Push! Push, Laura!" The doctor's instructions are so loud they bounce off the walls in the delivery room. To induce labor for a baby that hadn't moved in an hour, Dr. O'Brien had injected Laura with twice the dosage of Oxytocin. Two nurses are on each side of Laura holding her arms down. Another nurse is assisting Dr. O'Brien. The fetal heart monitors are faint, but Laura's heart monitor is beeping through the roof. The pain can only be described as hellish. The lower part of Laura's body feels like it has been dropped in a barrel of knives. Any movement only exacerbates the feeling. It's as if she is paralyzed with pain. The morphine has been stopped for fear of the fetus' lack of pulmonary activity. Laura's bowels have long since evacuated, and the other patients on the floor are silent as Laura's screams pierce the halls. Laura wishes she would die.

Paul can only watch the steady stream of nurses go in and out of the direction of the delivery room. Two nurses have exited, covered in sweat and blood.

Dr. O'Brien has her right hand pushing down on Laura's belly, trying to get this baby out. The doctor's left hand is by the large vaginal tear from which the baby's head protrudes. The baby is too large for Laura's hips, and the doctor wonders if she will live through this. The nurse is crouched down, ready to pull the baby out when enough of the head shows. When a baby is born, it is not normal for there to be no movement. There is almost a one hundred percent chance the baby has died when there is no movement.

Sweat soaked through the bed, and Laura was about to pass out from the pain and effort. The last thought she has before blacking out is regret. She can also make out something Dr. O'Brien says.

"Jesus Christ, it hit the floor."

When Laura blacked out, her muscles relaxed enough that the baby slipped out. It slipped out too fast for the doctor or the nurse to catch him. The baby's sound when it hit the tile floor was a sickening thud. They both swooped down to pick him up and check for vitals. He was alive, but his head struck the floor first. There was a silence and thick, humid quality to the air. Blood and fluid were everywhere. The two nurses on each side of Laura began to clean her up and try to revive her. The doctor cleaned and examined the crying child. She examines him for cephalohematoma. It's a needlessly long word to describe a blood hemorrhage in the brain. Dr. O'Brien hoped the swelling and the hemorrhaging would stop. The baby was quickly taken to the neonatal intensive care unit or N.I.C.U.

The nurse who tried to assist in the birth has tears in her eyes. Dr. O'Brien goes to the still-unconscious Laura and opens her eyes to see if they dilate. They do.

"He came out too fast. I couldn't catch him. I'm sorry. I'm so sorry."

"He's breathing. It's been known to happen. I'll stitch the mother up and then talk to the father. I want you to clean yourself up." The doctor puts a sympathetic hand on the devastated nurse's shoulder.

Most babies are placed on the mother's chest to get warm and for the heartbeats to synchronize. Some babies can immediately breastfeed. Laura's baby could not do any of these things. Low amniotic fluid triggered constriction of blood to the umbilical cord. The lack of blood flow caused low blood pressure in the baby and no movement in utero. He also suffered a head injury during birth and was whisked away to be monitored for the next seven days. The brain injury will reveal itself in adolescence with a slightly drooping left eye and a learning disability. He will never dream when he sleeps. He will grow up wondering why his peers tease him and make him cry. He will never fit in or ever realize his potential. His heart will harden and turn black. His own mother regrets his birth. Michael Anthony Phy was born on Friday, the eleventh of April, 1980.

Laura is still unconscious, and in this unconscious state, she dreams. It's a dream she will not remember. She is sitting in a small metal boat, nude, with her knees tucked under her chin. There is a fog around her, and the water the boat sits on is gray. The boat is listless, and there is no wind. A feeling of isolation, loss and dread overwhelm her. The fog dissipates, and a shoreline fifty feet away is revealed. A little girl in a white dress is waving to her. She is a brunette with pigtails and a round face. The girl is not waving hello, but goodbye. Laura looks up to see black clouds circling overhead, and the little girl is gone when she looks back to the shoreline.

While Laura dreams, Paul is standing over her. She is recovering in the intensive care unit. Paul's shadow covers Laura's face from the fluorescent light above. Paul studies her face, and she looks different, pale, aged, and withered. Part of Paul feels a twinge of anger toward her. He wished she was more accepting of the pregnancy. Maybe *she wouldn't be the wreck she is now if she was.* His thoughts are cold, and so is his touch on her arm, covered in bruises and tubes that feed her medicine to keep her hydrated and her heart pumping. Paul feels no guilt for getting a teenage girl pregnant. The thought never crossed his mind. Another part of Paul is happy. He has a son. It was the last time Paul would be proud of him.

Dr. Pam O'Brien is sitting in her office tonight. It was a long, terrible day. Her chair is turned away from her desk so she can see all her degrees on the wall. She removes her glasses and pinches the bridge of her nose. She cannot remember a more difficult delivery. The mother was slight, and her birth canal may have been too small, but it should not have been that treacherous. Dr. O'Brien could not shake the feeling that something was holding the baby in.

Some sort of force. The sound of the baby hitting the floor is something she cannot get out of her head. A baby slipping and falling in childbirth was rare but not unheard of. Her thoughts quickly drifted to Napa Valley in California. She had visited once about ten years ago and thought of retiring there. She had stayed in New Jersey too long. In the bottom drawer on the left side of her desk, under the lock and key, was a bottle of gin. Her deceased husband's drink of choice before lovemaking. He died five years ago after falling outside this hospital on a patch of ice. He was also a doctor and did not mention the fall to anyone. He simply drove home and went to sleep with a headache. He never woke up. A doctor should know better, but he was stubborn. Doctor Pam O'Brien should have left for California then, but she stayed. She felt she needed to keep working to keep her mind off her husband's death and to keep one foot going in front of the other. Now there were regrets. Tonight was for recollections aided by gin. in the morning, it would be her resignation.

Chapter 11

Summer and Fall, 1980

Freddy is on his way to Angela's home. "Brandy" by the band Looking Glass plays on the car radio. Warm day and the windows are open. Freddy feels good despite the heavy traffic headed eastbound on Route 37. Outsiders have started to come into town for the New Jersey shore. A routine had developed between Freddy and Angela recently. He would see her and Billy every other weekend and maybe twice during the week. When they are together, he notices that Angela does not talk about Tasha. He assumes they have arguments, and Angela does not want to discuss them with him. His plan was working and much quicker than he had even expected. Freddy also enjoyed time with Billy. The child seemed to light up when Freddy was around. He would take him outside and play while Angela would make lunch. Tasha was not home those days.

As Freddy neared Angela's place, he remembered a night just a month ago when she had asked him to babysit. Tasha was visiting family in Philadelphia, and Angela had to work. Freddy found it pretty basic. Keep the child safe, warm, clean and fed. Around eight in the evening, Billy began to cry. He was hungry. Freddy went to the refrigerator and got his bottle of breast milk. Before giving the bottle to Billy, he took a sip of Angela's breastmilk for himself. He was surprised to find out that it tasted like regular milk. After his sip, he noticed an uncooked steak still in the styrofoam and plastic wrapping at the bottom of the refrigerator. Blood had begun to pool around it. Freddy took the steak out and wiped the blood up in the fridge. Before cleaning the bloodied sponge, he had an idea. Freddy unscrewed the baby bottle's top and squeezed the sponge's blood into Billy's milk. It gave the milk a pink color. Freddy tossed the sponge in the sink, put the steak back in the refrigerator, and fed Billy the pink breast milk.

At Angela's trailer, he sees Angela on the front steps sobbing. Freddy gets out of his car and hurries to her.

"What happened? You okay?"

"Tasha left," Angela says with red, teary eyes.

Freddy begins to smile on the inside.

The night before, there was an argument. The arguing had gotten so loud that Frank McGovern, owner of Pine Acres Trailer Park, came out of his trailer to see if he needed to call the police. He didn't. He saw Tasha leaving the trailer, with bags packed, in a taxi cab. Frank had assumed Tasha and Angela were only friends and that friends sometimes fight. No one at Pine Acres thought they were a couple. Frank now worried if Angela could afford to live by herself.

Real estate lawyer Henry McGovern originally purchased Pine Acres in 1952. Henry was a well-respected lawyer and businessman in Toms River. He even flirted with a run for mayor but dropped out due to his alcoholism. His only son, Frank, was originally a property caretaker before taking over the day-to-day operations. Under Frank, the property flourished. Ten trailers ballooned to fifty, and the money coming in enabled Henry to retire to Florida in 1965. Frank stayed behind and ran Pine Acres by himself. He was never married and had no children. It was a lonely life for him, but the work was steady and kept him preoccupied.

Besides the property, Frank also inherited his father's taste for alcohol. In 1970 a near-fatal car accident downtown changed Frank's life. He almost killed a family of three, but an angel must have been on everyone's shoulder that night. Both cars were totaled, but no deaths.

Frank quit drinking cold turkey the very next day. He paid a fine and was without a driver's license for three years. Frank didn't serve jail time because of his last name in town. He stayed close to Pine Acres and kept himself out of trouble. Frank was now fifty-five years old and thinking of handing over some of the day-to-day operations of Pine Acres. Frank loved his job but loved the idea of retirement even more. He didn't want to sell the property to a bank for fear they would turn around and sell the land to a developer. Frank cared for his tenants. He knew they didn't have much, and the thought of them being kicked out of their homes was unthinkable. He pondered this while watching Tasha's taxi leave the property. His mood turned sullen, and he returned to his trailer in the middle of Pine Acres.

Frank first met Freddy Bile the day after Tasha had left. Frank didn't think much of him; he was squirrely looking, peculiar. Frank was over six feet tall, and Freddy was barely five feet tall with thick glasses and greasy hair. Frank couldn't figure out why Angela had taken a liking to him. Freddy filled out the necessary paperwork with Frank and moved into Angela's trailer the following week. Over the summer, Pine Acres started to look cleaner and tidier than before. Frank knew it was because of Freddy. He would see Freddy going around the property picking up trash, fixing damaged fences and doing maintenance on neighbor's trailers. Frank was curious about why Freddy was doing all this maintenance without compensation. He started a conversation with him, and Freddy told him he just enjoyed that kind of work since it was the same thing he did at the cemetery. A friendship between the two men just sort of happened. Frank found Freddy to be peculiar but also charming and a hard worker. He would sometimes watch Freddy playing with Billy outside. It all became very normal, and things in Pine Acres were quiet.

On Labor Day weekend, some residents had barbecues and family get togethers. It ended up looking like a big block party. The weather was perfect, and Frank watched it all from the front porch of the trailer. Freddy comes up to Frank with a beer.

"Enjoying the weather, Franklin?" Freddy says, attempting to hand Frank the beer.

"Don't drink. Thanks though. Been on the wagon now for ten years." Frank says, drinking his can of soda.

"Congratulations. Quite the milestone. More for me." Freddy says with a smile.

The two watch their neighbors celebrate the day. Angela is with Billy and watching him play with the other kids from the Pine Acres. Billy is grabbing the soapy bubbles a little girl is blowing around him.

"Going to be sad to leave here in a few years, but Florida is calling my name," Frank says.

"Who's going to run the place?" Freddy asks, intrigued.

"I've got a couple of ideas, but nothing set in stone."

"I'd be interested in throwing my hat in the ring."

"It would be a full-time job, Freddy. Aren't you exhausted from the cemetery?"

"I'm a workaholic. I've been self-sufficient since I was a child."

"Okay, I'll put you in the running, but it won't for a couple of years still," Frank says. He does like Freddy and is sure he would be a good replacement. He isn't sure if Freddy would be able to handle the financial aspect of the job. The labor part he has no qualms about. Frank had other suitors in mind. Tim Parsons had been a resident since 1955, and his wife Jean was a retired accountant. Then there was an old business partner of his father, John Rosetto of Rosetto Realty. He had expressed an interest in buying land in Toms River. Now, Freddy Bile was in consideration.

Freddy felt a new passion in his life at this very moment. His old passion, Angela, was playing with her son. His new passion was Pine Acres. As he sat drinking his beer, he began to envision plans for this property. He thought of the thousands of dollars coming in every single month, he thought of tax breaks, he thought of expansion, and he thought of control. He thought of private and isolated property with residents he hand-picked. The ones he didn't care for he could have evicted for whatever reason, but he would keep the ones he felt he could manipulate. Freddy now wanted Pine Acres for himself. He wanted a community all his own, and he wanted it now and not in two years. The only thing standing in the way of that was Frank McGovern.

That evening as fireworks lit up the sky over Pine Acres, Freddy sat with Angela and Billy outside, watching the colors blast. Summer was ending, and Freddy was never happier. He had a family that he wanted and a new goal to set his sights on. Angela pretended to be happy, but her thoughts drifted off to Tasha. She had worried for her and had not heard from her in two months. Billy was trying to touch the fireworks in the sky. Freddy watched Billy try to capture the magic overhead and watched the other Pine Acres residents enjoy the light show. He remembered something Frank had told him earlier. Plans were beginning to take shape in Freddy's mind. To get rid of Tasha, Freddy used the boy. To get rid of Frank, he will use Frank's alcoholism.

Poisoning someone without detection is very tricky. Slowly introducing a poison or toxin into someone's bloodstream in small doses can prevent detection. However, it can also build up the victim's tolerance to the poison or toxins. It is a sort of twisted irony that it is possible that the more you poison someone, the more immune you make them. The balance is finding the correct dose in the correct timeframe to achieve the desired result, which is death. Freddy Bile did not want to use poison on Franklin McGovern. He wanted to introduce alcohol into his bloodstream in small doses so Frank's body would start craving it again. Then Freddy would simply wait for Frank to binge on alcohol and die from its poisoning. When a heroin addict quits using and has flushed all of the toxins from their system, they can physically recover, but not mentally. Mentally they are still the same person. When they relapse, which is almost guaranteed, the person's mentality is that they can take the same amount of heroin they used before recovery. They cannot. Their body has not built up the tolerance for the drug, and when it is introduced again into the system in the amount the addict thinks it should be able to handle, the system simply shuts down, causing death. Freddy's plan is devious, calculated, and effective.

Three weeks had passed since Freddy had started lacing Frank's food with minute amounts of base liquors. Rum was put in his soda and snack foods. Vodka was put on the steaks he had in the freezer. Freddy had made copies of Frank's keys when Frank was fixing the roof on Mrs. Claxton's trailer after a rainstorm. When Frank wasn't home, Freddy would slip in with a syringe filled with whatever liquor Freddy chose and lace Frank's food. There were no noticeable differences in Frank's behavior until one morning in early October when Freddy knocked on Frank's door at eleven in the morning on a Saturday. Frank had overslept, and when he answered the door, Freddy could smell booze on his breath.

"You okay, Franklin? It's not like you to oversleep. We have to pick up mulch for Mr. Jennings' front garden today." Freddy says with a smile.

"That's today? Shit. Sorry, Freddy. You can go ahead. I'll help you in a bit. I don't feel good." Frank says, stumbling back into his trailer.

Freddy follows Frank inside and can see scattered bottles of gin and tequila, other base liquors Freddy had contemplated using.

"Not that it is any of my business Franklin, but I'm guessing you're not on the wagon anymore. Would I be correct in that assertion?"

"I fell off the wagon and did a goddamn somersault. Don't tell anyone, Freddy. I'm ashamed of this. If the other tenants found out, they'd overreact. Kick my ass outta here. I can beat this. I did before, and I can beat it again." Frank says while sitting with his head in his hands.

"I know you can. Your secret is safe with me." Freddy makes a motion as if he is zipping his mouth shut.

Freddy does keep Frank's secret from the other tenants at Pine Acres. They get curious when they see him less and less, and they see Freddy and Angela taking care of the property and its office work more and more. Over the fall, rumors begin to start. The rumors range from Frank drinking or that he is very sick and dying. Freddy does nothing to squash the rumors as he is busy running the day-to-day of the trailer park and his full-time job at the cemetery. Angela handles the rent collection and the phone in the main office. She checks on Frank in his trailer occasionally, but he is either sleeping or not there at all. Sometimes Frank slips into the backwoods behind Pine Acres with a bottle of vodka and isn't seen for a day or two. Angela's heart goes out to Frank, who has shown her nothing but kindness since she moved in. She sits in the main office cleaning up when Mrs. Claxton comes in without knocking.

"Thank God you're here." Mrs. Claxton says, out of breath.

"What is it? Something wrong?" Angela says, scared.

"My son Randy was hunting deer this morning in the woods behind us. He says he saw a dead body. He had a handgun next to him. He thinks he shot himself."

"Who is it?"

"Randy thinks it was Frank."

Angela hurries out of the office and sees Randy standing by his pickup truck.

"Take me to him. Randy. Mrs. Claxton, I want you to call the police." Angela and Randy hop in the truck, and Mrs. Claxton returns to the office.

On the way to the body, there are twists and bumps on the dirt trails leading cut into the woods.

"We should have gotten him help. That poor man." Angela says. Up ahead, she sees Freddy kneeling by a body on the ground. The truck stops, and Angela walks over slowly to Freddy.

"Don't look. It's bad. Call the police?"

"Mrs. Claxton did. It really is Frank?"

"Yes. I should have gotten his guns. I didn't think he was so depressed." Freddy says while still looking at what was left of Frank's face. Randy stands next to Freddy.

"What do we do now? Do we have to move? I don't want to sound cold, but he ran the place. I can't afford to live anywhere else." Randy says with his orange hunting cap clutched to his chest.

"Don't worry about such things, Randall. Angela and I run Pine Acres. We're not going anywhere." Freddy stands and puts his hand on Randy's shoulder. He walks to Angela and hugs her. Off in the distance, police and ambulance sirens can be heard. Freddy looks down at the ground and sees an empty bottle of vodka.

Chapter 12

Spring, 1981

To get lost in one's passion can be a glorious thing. It consumes your thoughts and

actions, gives you purpose, and makes your heart feel full. Freddy Bile never had those feelings

until he met Angela Mallek and her son William. He had them again months later when he took

control of the Pine Acres Trailer Park from Frank McGovern. Freddy was always the beta male

in life. He was the scrawny, weird, ex-mortician cemetery worker who lived alone on the

outskirts of town. Now, he felt like the alpha. He had a woman, a child who needed him, and the

hundred tenants at Pine Acres. Every day, his confidence grew - a far cry from his youth. Freddy

had unconsciously conceived of this community in those fragile and lonely times. His mother, a

blood donor for a small group of sanguinarians, gave him the first inklings of what he wanted. A

small, secret sect that operated under the noses of everyone else in town. Freddy wanted to start

his own sanguinarian community here at Pine Acres. To do that would take time. Most current

tenants were elderly or just young, poor families. To convert them to a lifestyle they had never

heard of would not happen easily. Freddy needed to wait until the elderly tenants died of old age

or were put in nursing homes. They were replaced by young drifters, miscreants, ex-convicts,

and recovering addicts. Freddy needed young people he could mold and manipulate. It would

take time, but time was all he had. For the new, more desirable tenants to afford to live at Pine

Acres, they were put on assignments by Freddy. The assignments included but were not limited

to, theft, prostitution, and narcotics. The trailer park became a small crime syndicate with Freddy

Bile as godfather.

Playing on the front porch with Billy on a warm April evening, Freddy looked out at the other trailers in Pine Acres. Freddy does not call it Pine Acres anymore. He refers to it only as the Community. Angela is lying on the couch inside, taking a nap before her shift at the Happy Hour. The two did not quit their regular jobs. They needed to keep up appearances and keep their eyes and questions about the trailer park to a minimum. Local businesses within a two-mile radius of the Community had recent break-ins, and authorities had been notified. A police cruiser would sometimes come through Pine Acres at odd night hours. Freddy had noticed. A laundromat in Lakehurst had been broken into, and money was taken from the coin-operated machines. Thousands of dollars in damage, and the owner of the laundromat knew it was the work of the "white trash" living in Pine Acres. He promptly closed up shop and moved to Lacey Township, five miles down the road. The spike in crime in the area had not gone unnoticed by the Toms River Police Department.

Officer Clarence Gardener was a fifteen-year veteran on the force, one of the few black police officers that Toms River had produced. He would patrol Pine Acres from time to time and have heard the rumors of this place being the home to many unsavory characters. Clarence fixated on the new proprietor, Frederick Bile. He knew him from Riverside Cemetery as he handled the burials of retired and or officer killed-in-action. Clarence would park his cruiser across the road and watch. He found it strange that most activity and traffic in Pine Acres was quiet in the day but got busier under cover of darkness. Cars and pickup trucks went in and out after sundown. Clarence would sometimes joke about dispatching that the tenants behaved like vampires.

The traffic in the Community did increase at night. It made it difficult for Angela to get any sleep before work. Freddy had thought she was napping, but she couldn't. She was restless. Angela was happy to be with Freddy, even if the relationship was hardly romantic. To Angela, it was more of an arrangement. They lived like a couple, ran the park together, raised Billy, and would even occasionally have intercourse, but there was no deep connection for Angela. Angela's love was for someone else. Freddy's love was all here in the Community. Angela got up from the couch and walked to the back window to see Freddy sitting out back with Billy on his lap. The image is a stark contrast to what her life was months ago with Tasha. Seeing a man with Billy did give her a sense of normalcy. It also made her uneasy.

A week later, with Angela at work and Billy asleep, Freddy sits in the living room with Sam Betancourt. Sam had a garbage bag full of cash for Freddy in different denominations.

"That cop keeps coming through here," Sam says.

"I'm aware of that, Samuel. Just have the drop-offs in the woods behind us. Tell our runners to stick to the dirt trails."

Sam Betancourt was released from prison eight months ago and needed a place to stay. He struck up a friendship with Freddy at the Happy Hour. After a vetting process, which amounted to a series of questions, Freddy invited Sam to move into the Community. He was in his mid-forties, tall, with dark hair and a handlebar mustache. He was a biker. Sam had served ten years in New Jersey State Prison for armed robbery. In his youth, he had multiple assault and weapons charges. Sam had been in and out of prison at least four times. He could have been viewed as a liability for Freddy, but Freddy needed his connections to the underground types in town. To Freddy, Sam would never turn. He would do time before talking. That's why Sam Betancourt became Freddy's right hand in the Community. He was also not religious, which is unusual since many ex-cons find God while incarcerated. Sam might be more open to Freddy's other tastes.

The idea of drinking blood for sustenance, not for pleasure, was floated by Freddy to Sam over beers at the Happy Hour a week before Sam moved to the Community.

"Blood? You mean human blood?" Sam asks.

"We work up to that. All it is really is a lifestyle choice. You feel stronger, younger, and more connected. I do it only on occasion for health reasons. It's nothing you can force on someone." Freddy tells Sam while drinking his beer.

"Does Angela do this?"

"No, but I'll win her over. It's just something for you to think about, Samuel. Who knows? You might actually like it." Freddy smiles. Sam just finished his beer.

Now as they sit in Freddy's trailer counting the bag of cash, Freddy wonders how to get Sam on board with becoming a blood drinker.

"How do you like your hamburger, Samuel?"

"Are you going to make us hamburgers? I'm hungry. Rare."

"Rare? So you do drink blood. You just didn't know it."

"Not the same thing, Freddy."

"You ingest it all the same. It's not such a leap. There's a glass in the refrigerator. Take a sip. It's from a deer Randall Claxton shot two days ago." Freddy says to Sam. He stopped counting the money and stared at Sam over the top of his glasses that slipped down his nose. Sam felt Freddy was not asking this time.

"Sip?"

"Nothing more."

Sam gets up and goes to the refrigerator. He opens the door, and sitting in the middle is a large glass of a deer's red, brown blood. Sam takes it over to the couch in front of Freddy. The glass being cold doesn't help the cause. The idea of drinking cold animal blood was not how Sam saw this night going, which turned his stomach.

"Get it over with, Samuel," Freddy says, beginning to count the money again.

Sam takes the glass and takes a sip. He nearly gags at the cold, syrup-metallic taste. He swallows.

"That wasn't so bad now, was it?" Freddy didn't look up from the money.

"Am I a member now?" Sam asks, hoping not to drink anymore.

"Now you are." Freddy looks up and smiles at Sam.

Trying not to vomit in front of Freddy, Sam thinks of why he is here. Freddy had given Sam shelter, a job, money, and the prospect of earning more. Freddy even floated the idea of expansion into other states like Pennsylvania and upstate New York. He needed men he could trust. Sam wanted to be trustworthy. Small-time stuff like lifting cars or selling pot was one thing, but the idea of this cult and drinking blood was another. While in prison, you associate with types you would rather avoid, but you do what you have to to stay alive. Sam needed to stay alive outside prison walls, so he toed the line with the Community even if it meant becoming a sanguinarian. He takes another sip and controls his gag reflex.

"The tricks in Seaside are making good money, but the fucking cops are scaring the shit out of the younger ones," Sam says, struggling to swallow the blood. He worries about being busted, and the black cop that parks across the way aren't helping his nerves.

"Don't put them on the streets. Tell them to work the bars and hotel lobbies. How's the parts business? We should double this amount." Freddy is almost finished counting the money.

"It'll get there. It's tough finding a dishonest mechanic. Can you believe that?" Sam chuckles to himself. The car parts business was very simple. Stealing mufflers, catalytic converters, batteries, headlights, whatever was quick and easy to swipe and then selling them for a tiny profit to dishonest mechanics and junkyards in town so they, in turn, could sell back to the public at whatever price they wanted. The problem was that Toms River was a small town, and being caught with stolen merchandise could shut a shop down.

"I know a mechanic. Paul Phy in the downtown area. Born here. He knows every mechanic and chop shop in this town and others. Talk to him tomorrow. Tell him you're a friend of mine."

"Done." Sam is impressed with the solutions Freddy has. Sam was leery of Freddy Bile at first, but now he sees that he has brains. Sam respected that.

Monday morning at Phy's Garage was busier than usual. Paul has been spending more time at the garage lately, and work has been coming in steadily. Paul has his head under the hood of a Chevrolet Impala when Sam Betancourt pulls up in front of the shop. Paul peeks out from under the hood and sees Sam walk through the open garage door.

"Are you Paul Phy?"

"I am."

"I'm a friend of Fred Bile. Says he knows you."

"I know, Freddy. What can I do for you?" Paul wipes the grease from his hands with a shop towel and offers a handshake.

"I'm Sam, and I have some merchandise Freddy says you might be interested in. Got it in the back of my truck. Take a gander if you like."

"Sure." Paul follows Sam to the back of Sam's pickup. He pulls a sheet off some car parts in his truck bed.

"I'm going to guess that these aren't yours?" Paul asks.

"Be surprised what you can find if you look hard enough," Sam says with a smile.

"I'll take it all. Pull around back and unload it for me."

"All of it? Right now?"

"No time like the present. Tell Freddy I said thanks. I could move this stuff pretty quick."

Sam takes the pickup to the back of Paul's shop. Pallets, steel drums, tires, and two rusted-out motors complete the look. Sam starts to unload the batteries, mufflers, and converters.

"I guess we need to talk about money," Sam says.

"Fifteen items, plus your time, how's four hundred?" Paul asks.

"Freddy told me to take your first offer as a show of faith. Four hundred it is."

Paul takes out a wad of cash from his back pocket and counts out the four hundred in fifty dollar bills. He gives it to Sam.

"I wish they could all be this easy, Mr. Phy. There's plenty more where that came from."

"How is Freddy? Haven't seen him in a while."

"Keeping busy. He took over the trailer park, so most of his time is spent there."

"He did? Wonder why he did that. Tell him I said hello." Paul shakes Sam's hand. Sam's pickup pulls out from the shop, and Paul looks down at the parts he just purchased.

What are you up to, Freddy? Paul wonders. He goes back inside and under the hood of the Chevrolet. He feels more comfortable here than at home. His son Michael is turning one next week. One year has felt like ten. Laura has been a stay-at-home mother, and she is not enjoying it. She has two moods, one is combative, and the other is sullen. Paul didn't know which he would come home to. Paul and Laura did not know she was suffering from long and severe postpartum depression.

Michael is crying in his crib. At one year, most infants can walk, say a few words, find toys, and understand yes and no from a parent. Michael can do none of these things. He has been regulated to his crib most of his young life. The consequences of the lack of development will be felt later. Laura is sitting on the sofa near the crib, silhouetted by the sunlight coming in through a window. She is smoking a cigarette and lost in her thoughts, oblivious to Michael's constant crying and uncaring about what the secondhand smoke might be doing to her child's lungs. Her thoughts range from a cavalcade of chores yet to be started, the longing for a daughter and her mother never calling. That isn't entirely true, her mother did call over Christmas, but that was all. Laura hardly thought of Paul. When she did, it was accompanied by a sharp pain in her stomach - a sort of muscle memory sensation. She associated that nightmarish birth a year ago with him. There was still time for a daughter, but Laura did not want Paul to be the father. The thoughts stop when Laura realizes the baby is crying. She doesn't attempt to comfort the baby. The easiest way to make the baby stop would be to *smother it.* Laura quickly pushed that thought aside. She puts her cigarette in the ashtray next to her and walks over to Michael. Her eyes lift to the next room. She stares at the kitchen sink and then back to Michael. Another thought was quickly dismissed. Laying him down now and covering him with a blanket doesn't stop the crying, but it gives Laura a moment to feel that she tried. She turns to look out the window and sees Paul pulling into the driveway. Laura leaves for the kitchen with Michael still whimpering and starts dinner.

Chapter 13

May, 1987

Yellowjacket wasps are sometimes confused with bees because of their color, stingers, and similarities in colony behavior. Colonies consist of workers, drones and queens. Nests are set up in trees, old logs, underground, and warm man made structures like old barns, decks and sheds. The queen remains inside to fertilize the eggs while the workers, all female, expand the nest and gather food. The drones, all male, are simply around to mate and die. A colony can expand to as many as 5,000 wasps, but they only last one season until the winter and die. They are efficient, evolved, and cold. For the colony to survive, it must have one queen. If multiple queens are in one colony, they fight until only one remains. If the worker bees accept the queen, all is well, but if they reject the queen, the workers surround her until she overheats and dies.

The colony under Paul's deck is the size of a softball. A soldier is out because she can sense and smell sugar. She is out from under the deck and hovering over Michael, who is now seven years old and eating a chocolate ice cream cone. He is sitting and playing with plastic, little green army men. The heat from the sun makes sweat drip down the back of Michael's neck. He wipes the sweat away with his chocolate-covered fingers. The scent is too much to resist for the soldier wasp. She lands on Michael's shoulder and begins to crawl to the back of his neck. She slowly moves under the collar of his "He-Man" t-shirt. Michael can feel something under his shirt, so he slaps at the back of his neck. It was nothing at first, then a stabbing pain shot between his shoulder blades. He panics and screams and drops his ice cream. He pulls off his shirt, and the soldier flies off. Michael begins wailing and runs into the house. He runs past Paul, who is watching the Yankees game on television. Paul attempts to attend to his son, but Michael runs to his mother in the kitchen. Laura sees Michael, red-faced and shirtless screaming in pain.

"What happened?" Laura gets up from cleaning the oven.

"I got stung." Michael turns so his mother can see his back. She can see a red welt between his shoulder blades.

"You sure did. Come on." She takes his hand and takes him to the bathroom. Paul never gets up from the couch. Laura doesn't know if Michael is allergic to bee or wasp stings. She doesn't know if he's allergic to anything.

A half-hour later, Michael is lying in bed on his side. The tears have dried, but the throbbing is still persistent on his back. A breeze comes in through his open bedroom window, and he can hear his mother in the kitchen. She is listening to the Beach Boys "In My Room." Michael begins to feel sad. A sort of sadness that comes from loss. His mother and father had not consoled him the way he expected. His mother put some antiseptic and a band-aid, but that was all. There was no hug or kiss on the forehead. The pain from the sting was still there and not fading. What was fading was Michael's sense of importance in his parent's eyes. His father didn't even bother to check on him. *Maybe they don't love me anymore.* He thinks. There is a point in a child's life when they realize that the world does not revolve around them. It can range from a beating from a parent or being humiliated by them in front of others. It can also be as simple as meeting another child with the same name. They realize they don't even have sole ownership of their name. They begin to feel less special. They let go of that feeling that it is too much. Some children might gravitate to a favorite blanket or toy and hold on to it for years. It keeps them in a childlike state. They will eventually have to outgrow these attachments. Michael didn't have a favorite blanket or toy, so he decided to hold on to the pain of the wasp sting. The searing pain will be his safety blanket. It's something he will never outgrow. He will keep it with him for the rest of his life. It will remind him of the day he began to hate his parents.

Chapter 14

Summer, 1987

Rebecca Bailey was born on January 3rd, 1970, in Sayreville, New Jersey. Her parents, Tim and June Bailey, reported her missing on May 7th, 1987. Her childhood was fairly normal and loving. There were birthday parties, toys at Christmas, plenty of friends at school and after-school activities. She was pretty and got the attention of boys at an early age. She was smart and excelled in class. Her parents were very proud of their daughter. She was an only child, which explains why Tim and June were strict with her. Rebecca wasn't allowed out on Saturday nights, and she wasn't allowed to date boys without a parent present. Her schedule was regimented. School is Monday through Friday, with cheer practice after. She was allowed to have a friend over on Saturday, and Sunday was for church and family. When Rebecca turned fifteen, she longed to have more freedom. She felt she had earned it with her consistent placement on the honor roll, and even a few colleges had taken notice of her 4.0-grade point average as a sophomore. Rebecca wanted a boyfriend and to go to parties to make new friends.

Rebecca skipped class in November 1985 to go to Billy Porter's house. His parents were at work. The two smoked cigarettes and drank in his basement. After a beer and a half, Rebecca was drunk, and Billy started to remove his clothes. Rebecca remembers the awkwardness and pain of her first time and how she tried to stop Billy. He held her down and pushed into her. After a few minutes, it was over. The moments after were a bit of a blur as clothes were put back on, and Billy hurriedly walked her home. Rebecca immediately felt ashamed and went to the bathroom to throw up and take a shower. She told her parents she had an upset stomach.

The next day at school, she heard whispers behind her back. "Blowjob, Becky," a girl said in the hallway. One word that stuck in her heart was "slut" which came from a boy on her school bus. When Rebecca confronted Billy the next day about why he had spread rumors about her, he denied it and even denied knowing her. She was crushed, and Rebecca's parents noticed an immediate change. Her grades suffered, and she quit the cheerleading squad. She skipped more and more classes and began to hang out with a different crowd. When her parents could smell marijuana on her, they threatened to kick her out and send her to North Carolina to live with her grandparents on her father's side. The idea was that a drastic move away from bad influences would straighten her out.

The downward spiral went on like this for a while, and on May 4th of 1987, Rebecca came home after being missing for an entire weekend and had a terrible fight with her mother. Yelling at first and then some harsh words. It escalated, and Rebecca slapped her mother. Shocked and fearful, June told her daughter to leave. Rebecca gathered her things and made a phone call. Forty-five minutes later, she got into a car with a young man her mother had never seen before. It was a man Rebecca met on the weekend down at the shore. His name was Randy Claxton.

Randy was driving with a tearful Rebecca in the passenger seat. Randy had to look sad and match Rebecca's mood. He wanted to console her and be someone she could confide in. He needed to gain her trust for what was to come. The whole time, however, all Randy could think about was telling Freddy and Sam that he had found the girl.

"Don't worry about anything, Becky. I'll take you to a nice place. People are really nice there. You'll like it. Cheap too. The owner will find you work, so you don't have to worry about that." Randy says reassuringly.

"What kind of place?" Rebecca asks.

"Trailer park in Toms River. By the shore. Lots of young people are starting to move in there, so you'll fit right in. The owner, Freddy, he's a good man."

"It's only temporary. My home is Sayreville."

"Well, just give it a chance."

Randy's truck gets on the entrance ramp going south on the Garden State Parkway.

Tim and June had discussed options that night. They figured Rebecca would cool off and return home in a day or two. After three days, they started to worry. Friends had not heard from or seen her since the day she left. The man in the pickup truck was a stranger to everyone she knew. They had decided to call the police.

Randy and Rebecca had met by chance at a rest stop in South Amboy, New Jersey, on May 3rd. Rebecca had been in New York City with some friends trying to get into punk rock clubs with little to no success. At the rest stop, her friends went inside to use the bathroom and buy some food, but Rebecca remained in the car with the windows open. Randy pulled up next to her, and seeing a pretty teenage girl half asleep in a car, he decided to strike up a conversation. Randy was thin, with some tats and to Rebecca, he seemed a little trashy but cute in an edgy way. He was polite and wrote his number down on a piece of paper.

"Ever down by the shore, I can show you around."

"I used to go every summer as a kid." She said while folding the paper.

After the fight with her mother, Rebecca could only think to call Randy, the man from the rest stop. Randy had been at the rest stop because he was coming from upstate New York. He had dropped Sam Betancourt off at a property the Community had put a down payment on.

Pulling into Pine Acres, Rebecca saw all the mobile homes and started to feel homesick. Going from a nice suburban house to a trailer park in a town she wasn't very familiar with was overwhelming and a culture shock.

"I don't know, Randy. Maybe I should go home." Rebecca said, looking out the window at all the trailers.

"We got one at the end of this road that you can have. If you don't like it, you can always leave." Randy says, driving slowly to the end of the road. A plain white trailer sat by the door with an unpainted wooden deck and an empty flower pot.

"I don't have the money for this? What's the rent?" Rebecca asks.

"Just come on in and take a look." Randy parks in front, the two get out, and Rebecca follows Randy to the front door. A key is already sitting in the lock.

"You do the honors, Becky."

Rebecca turns the key, and she walks into the trailer. It's clean, quiet and empty.

"Two bedrooms, kitchen, bathroom, and washer. No dryer, you'd have to hang your clothes on the clothesline out back. Take a look around."

Rebecca begins to walk from room to room, but the idea of this being hers doesn't feel real. Being seventeen and never owning anything significant in her life, Rebecca worries about how much this will cost and why this stranger is so kind.

"What's the catch, Randy?"

When Rebecca turns to get an answer from Randy, she sees another man standing in the front doorway. She sees this slight, small man with his hair plastered down and thick-rimmed glasses.

"Hello Rebecca, welcome to the Community. My name is Frederick Bile, but you can call me Freddy."

"Nice to meet you, Freddy. Are you the manager?"

"I am, and so is my girlfriend, Angela. You can meet her later. She is sleeping now. The furniture here is up to you, but I think you will find the space comfortable. In terms of monthly rent, we can pick that up for you the first month until you get settled."

"That's what I'm unclear about. I can't pay for any of this. The trailer or the rent."

"You'll be working on the shore. Randy will explain the job to you. I have to go. It was nice meeting you, Rebecca." Freddy turns and leaves. Rebecca turns to Randy.

"The shore? Like at an arcade or something?"

"Hotels," Randy says, not wanting to make eye contact. He knows she will not like what he says next. "You will be going on dates with men in the area. What happens on these dates is up to you, but the more you do, the more you make. Half of what you make goes to Freddy. That's how you pay off this place."

"Dates? You mean like a hooker?" Rebecca asks.

"Think of it more like a companion for the evening."

"I gotta go. I knew this was too good to be true." Rebecca makes her way to the door, but Randy cuts her off.

"There is another way to pay this place off."

"I'm not interested, and please move." Rebecca feels threatened until Randy steps aside. She exits the trailer.

"Where will you go? Your parents don't want you. There's nothing up there for you. Down here, you can start a new life and make your own money. In time you can do something else, but I don't see you have a lot of options right now, Becky. You can be making hundreds a night. Every night." Randy watches Rebecca stop walking from him.

"Hundreds?" She asks.

"Every day. It depends on how hard you want to work."

Rebecca stands in between the trailer and Randy's truck. Part of her tells her to leave and get to a bus station. The other part tells her to try this. It all hinges on money and independence. At home, she has none, but here she may. She knows this. The decision she makes is important. It's a decision she will come to regret later.

August, on the boardwalk in Seaside Heights, is busy at all hours. Senior citizens enjoy the exercise and sun. Families enjoy the beaches, the games, and restaurants. Single people enjoy the bars. Rebecca is in the lobby of the Sun Motel. The management at the motel does not bother her because Freddy pays them to look the other way. Rebecca sits with a bathing suit top, cut-off jeans, and sandals. She is flipping through a teen magazine, waiting for single men to walk in. Most men she sees are tourists, college kids on break, or older regulars.

The room she uses is paid for the whole week, and most of her time is spent waiting. The appointments are not very long. Most just want to get in and out, fearing police knocking on the door or another local spotting them. Half hours are twenty-five dollars, hours are fifty, and anymore is one hundred. Rebecca is young and attractive, and the summer has been busy. On her best night, she took home five hundred and one hundred fifty on her worst. It was still more money than she had ever made before. Randy would show up or Sam when he wasn't in upstate New York if anyone got rough or out of line, but Freddy never stepped foot in the shore towns. On her days off, Rebecca would fix up her trailer, drink, and smoke pot with the others in the Community. She had gotten closer to Randy, but it never amounted to anything more than flirting. One night he mentioned wanting to drink her blood, but she tossed it off as him just being high. It wasn't until she overheard Freddy talking about his mother at a barbecue that she

started to wonder. "Blood donor" was the word he used to describe her, and something called

"sanguinarian." Rebecca never bothered to ask what that meant. Outside the lobby doors and

pacing on the sidewalk is a man in his sixties. He seems nervous, and Rebecca knows it's her

next appointment. She sighs and leaves the lobby to meet him outside.

"Come in if you're coming in. Don't worry. I won't bite."

"Oh, okay. Becky, right?"

"In the flesh. Come on. I'll show you a good time." Rebecca leads the man into the lobby

and up to the second floor to room 212.

Life was this way for Rebecca, and she began to tire of it. She wanted more for herself,

and the time she spent around kids at Pine Acres reaffirmed that she wanted to be a mother. She

was particularly fond of eight-year-old Billy Mallek. He always rode his bike to her trailer and

wanted to play hide and seek or tag with her. His black hair and big blue eyes were too much for

her to resist, so that she would play along. Rebecca had wanted to go home at the end of summer

and start a life for herself. She would have to complete school, find part-time work, and mend the

fences with her parents. Randy and Freddy agreed and promised they would help her get back

home. She had called her parents from pay phones near convenience stores because her trailer

did not have a landline. Freddy told her not to reveal her whereabouts to her family. Since he was

paying for her rent, she had agreed to that. She understood that Freddy was very secretive about

how the Community made its money. She even lied to her parents and said she was staying in

Atlantic City.

The next night Rebecca started packing up her trailer. Nothing big, just small items in

anticipation of the move in a few weeks. Angela is helping her. She had gotten to like Rebecca very much. "Words" by Missing persons is playing on the kitchen radio. She had let her babysit Billy some nights while she was bartending.

"Going to miss you, girl," Angela says while folding some of Rebecca's clothes.

"I'll miss you too. I'll come back down to visit. You're all like my second family here." Rebecca looks up to Angela like an older sister and role model for how she will handle motherhood.

"Freddy will miss you, and I know Randy definitely will."

"I know. Randy is too sweet. Who can tell the future, but I gotta concentrate on myself, you know."

"I've been there, Beck. You need to fix things with your folks. Family is the most important thing. Just no babies until you're ready. Then the sky's the limit. I love my boy, but I had him way too young."

"He's just too precious. What do you think is a good age to have a baby?"

"Not nineteen. Just wait until you know it's right."

"When I find the right guy, you mean? Like you and Freddy?"

"Sure. Like Freddy and I." Angela says halfheartedly. She has a flash of Tasha in her mind, but it quickly passes when there is a knock on the door. Rebecca answers it, and Randy is covered in sweat.

"What have you been doing? Come in."

"New project behind the property. I'm all dirty. I don't want to mess up your floors." Randy says, catching his breath.

"So, what's up?"

"Is there any way that we can change your mind about leaving? Not too late."

"No, it's time. I'm not leaving for another month, but I have to fix things at home."

"Well, we're all going to miss you. Especially Angela." Randy looks at Angela.

"That is the truth, but a woman's gotta do what she's gotta do."

"Yeah, alright, I'll leave you two ladies be." Randy turns to leave.

"What kind of project are you working on?" Rebecca asks.

"Oh, just some storage for the tenants. I'll see you later." Randy leaves, and Rebecca exchanges a quizzical look with Angela.

"Not sure what that was about."

"I think he's just got a thing for you. He's going to be like a lost puppy." Angela is trying to put Rebecca's mind at ease even though Angela has the same suspicions about Randy and Freddy. The Community is all-important to Freddy, and Rebecca knows how it finances itself. Freddy won't just let Rebecca leave.

Freddy had purchased a used ten-by-ten-foot metal storage container. A flatbed truck had brought it to Pine Acres three days ago. Freddy and Randy guided the flatbed to drop it deep in the backwoods behind the trailer park. The trucker was unhappy but consented to an extra two hundred dollars. Randy operated a backhoe to dig deep into the soft, sandy soil and, with chains, lowered the container into the ground. The only way into the container was through a circular opening fashioned by Randy and a jigsaw. A metal ladder was placed to get in and out. A mattress with three lanterns completed the furnishings inside, and the opening was covered with two layers of plywood. The dirt and sand were put back over the container concealing it from prying eyes. This was the project that Randy had been working on. A vision dreamt of by Freddy while logging all those long hours in the cemetery. Freddy knows how to bury things, and this thing will be Rebecca's tomb.

On Friday, August 29th, there was a party at Pine Acres. All the members of the Community gathered to send off Rebecca with lots of food, alcohol, weed, and laughter. It started in the morning and lasted all day Friday and into the early morning of Saturday the 30th.

"I'm going to miss you, baby. Stay in touch." Angela says while hugging Rebecca.

"Miss you too. I need a nap, shower, and rent a car. Too much to do, but that's what I get for procrastinating. Kiss Billy goodbye for me."

"I will." A quick kiss on the cheek to Rebecca.

Rebecca is buzzing from the party and staggers back to her trailer for the last time. Inside, she closes the door and waiting for her is Randy.

"Have fun? Hope so."

"I did. Randy, why are you here? I thought you went to your place."

Rebecca is confused as Randy walks to her. Randy moves in to kiss her, but she steps back. He smiles with a tear coming down his cheek.

"What are you doing?" Rebecca reaches behind her for the doorknob, but Randy grabs her arms and pulls her in. He kisses her, but she is not reciprocating. Rebecca feels attacked and tries to wiggle free, but Randy is too strong. He pushes her hard against the door, and the back of Rebecca's head strikes it. She is dazed, and the last thing she sees is Randy pulling a white handkerchief from his back pocket and putting it over her nose and mouth.

When Rebecca wakes, she can't open her eyes. She is nauseous and has a pounding headache. Her eyes are slightly open to see a flicker of dim orange and yellow light. She is naked and lying down on a mattress. Her wrists and ankles are tied together with ripped bedsheets. She begins to panic and moan as loud as she can. She is too weak to scream. She can roll off the mattress and feels the hard, cold metal floor under her.

"You should stay in bed."

"Where am I? What are you doing?" She asks.

Randy and Freddy emerge from the dark corner of the metal unit into the dim lantern light.

"You're very special to us, Rebecca. Randall found you and brought you here to us for a reason. I want you to take great pleasure in that you will provide a service to not only me but to all of us in the Community. There is nothing to worry about. Consider yourself as transcendent. Your essence will be in all of us now. Which means you will live on in all of us. My mother gave her body over to her people, and you will give your body over to your people. Your blood is precious and will sustain us." Freddy says. He motions to Randy. Randy bends down and places Rebecca back on the mattress. Freddy hands him a small pocket knife.

"What the fuck are you doing? Help!" Randy muzzles her screams with a rag. He opens the knife and begins lightly tracing it up her leg. He makes a small one-inch cut on her left thigh. Rebecca dares not struggle for fear the knife will be plunged into her. A light trickle of blood pushes out, and Randy begins to suck on the wound. After a minute, it is Freddy's turn.

"Thank you for your sacrifice," Freddy says after he swallows her blood.

Late afternoon Saturday, Angela and Billy went to Rebecca's trailer for a final goodbye, but the trailer was empty. Angela assumes she just missed her.

"I guess she left. I'm sure she will call us soon."

"She went back to her mom and dad?"

"Yes, baby. She will be safe at home. Come on. I have to start dinner."

Angela and Billy leave the trailer. Angela is unsure what to make of Rebecca leaving without a word, but Billy breaks her thoughts.

"Can we have pizza?"

"You don't like my cooking?"

Billy laughs, and so does Angela. She gives one last look back at Rebecca's now empty trailer.

After one week of being held captive without food, Rebecca is nearing death. Malnourished, dehydrated, and only two-thirds of her blood remains. She is too weak and delirious to try and escape. Senior members of the Community have been allowed to feed on her. Freddy has personally chosen them, and they have been sworn to secrecy. Other members of the Community, especially Angela, have been excluded for fear of them going to the authorities. Freddy loves his members but does not trust them implicitly, including Angela.

As Rebecca slips in and out of consciousness, she dreams of children. At a carnival, little boys and girls wonder at the clowns, animals, rides, and candy. The candy they cannot get enough of. Taffy and cotton candy are the children's favorites. They are ravenous for it, have sticky remnants all over their faces, and lick their lips and fingers. When Rebecca wakes, she can see, through her half-open eyes, an elderly couple from the community sucking the blood from each of her breasts. The blood is all over their faces and fingers. She is numb now and just wants to sleep, and she does. It will be the last sleep she will ever have. Her heart slows, and a high pitch noise rings in her ears. Her brain is shutting down, and there is no white light, only a sinking sensation similar to being anesthetized. Rebecca Bailey passed away on September the fourth, 1987.

Tim and June Bailey had reported their daughter missing four months prior, but the police had no leads. The phone calls she made to her home were from random pay phones around Toms River. Her photos from the missing posters in town were largely ignored, and she was never arrested or fingerprinted. She was considered another teenage runaway who would eventually be found. Her remains would not be discovered for another eleven years.

Chapter 15

February, 1998

Tasha is sitting at her kitchen table wearing aqua-blue nursing scrubs. She is slowly drinking her coffee while flipping through a book about different dog breeds. Nothing brings smiles to the faces of the old and sick like a baby or a dog. Tasha is thinking of getting something small to take to work to cheer up the elderly on her floor. Tasha Higgins was the Unit Manager of the Hampton Ridge Healthcare and Rehabilitation home in Toms River. She has held that position for the last five years. It was a far cry from where she was when she left Angela in the summer of 1980.

Eighteen years ago, she was broke, homeless and heartbroken. Tasha had hit rock bottom. She had been down before but had Priest to look after her. After Priest, she had Angela, but then Freddy took her away. The first thing Tasha needed was a roof over her head. She took what little money she had and got a room at the American Motel on Route 9 in Toms River. It was a dive motel, but she knew the manager. She had connections to pot dealers in Lakewood, one town over, and the manager took advantage of that. As long as the weed came in and it was of good quality, she could stay. It was the smallest room in the motel and had no hot water, but Tasha was happy to have a bed. The second thing on the list was money. A laundromat down the street was looking for someone part-time to sweep up, count receipts, and order parts for the broken-down washers and dryers. It was owned by a Hindi immigrant who took pity on Tasha and gave her a chance. She was never late, her counts were never off, and the machines were never down.

At night Tasha would think of Angela and Billy and cry herself to sleep, but over the months, she thought of them less and less. She made a conscious effort never ever to pass that part of town again. If she did, the memories would come flooding back, and the pain would be too much. Love and relationships would have to wait for now, if not for good. Third on the list for Tasha was going back to school. The laundromat was not a long-term solution. She had gotten her general equivalency in 1983, and after saving enough money, she applied for a nursing program at a vocational school. Tasha looked at the trends in town and saw a growing senior citizen population, so it made sense to look at a future career in nursing homes.

After getting her certification in 1988, she secured a job at St. Barnabas Healthcare facility as a trainee. The pay was meager but had room for advancement. She left the motel and got a very small one-bedroom apartment. In the three years at St. Barnabas, Tasha never called out and was never late. By 1993 she was offered a position at Hampton Ridge to oversee an entire floor. Tasha jumped at the chance and continued to excel. Tasha felt truly blessed and had a sense of pride for the first time in her life. The confidence she gained was miraculous. The spark happened in 1983 while walking home from the laundromat.

Tasha was tired from counting the laundromat's receipt tickets and the lack of a good night's sleep in her tiny bed at the American Motel. She was walking to the motel and always would go past a church. It was a large, gray, stone cathedral called the Church of Grace and Peace. It was a nondenominational church. Tasha hadn't gone to service since she was a girl in Philadelphia, but this cold night in January 1983 gave her pause. She thought, what would be the harm in attending just one mass? Her being gay did present problems. A Baptist church wouldn't take her in, nor would a Catholic one, but a nondenominational church she thought might be more open. She kept her sexuality to herself just in case it wasn't.

The following Sunday, after attending her first mass in years, Tasha walked out into the cold January night and felt different. Her head wasn't down but up, looking at the scattered snowflakes coming down. She breathed in the clean and cold air. She didn't feel cold but felt warm with a loving feeling. It wasn't the love she had for Angela. It was different, a universal sort of love. It was belonging to something of significance. Tasha wanted to cut poisonous ties from her life and start living. Everything needed to change if she wanted to become the woman she knew she could be. The reason she knew she could was simple.

"God was by my side." She would say to a friend or colleague when asked.

Now as she flipped through the pictures of dog breeds in the home she qualified to purchase herself, she stopped and looked up at a wooden crucifix she had up above the entrance to her kitchen. She then looked back at the book and decided on a Yorkshire terrier. She would pick one up the next day at a local shelter and name her Angel. The dog was six months old and weighed four pounds. It would yelp and lick Tasha's face when she picked her up. The patients on her floor loved Angel and would pet her and secretly give her candy or scraps of food when a nurse on call wasn't looking. The mood on the floor instantly improved, and even the surliest of patients couldn't help a little smile when Angel would strut on by their room. It made the nurse's job on the floor a little easier and provided a much-needed distraction from the normal day in day out routine. Tasha would take Angel home at night and let her sleep in the bed with her. She was the closest thing to a family member that Tasha had. Tasha never connected that the name Angel was derived from Angela.

Chapter 16

March, 1998

It is late afternoon, and the classroom is quiet. The last bit of winter is still holding on, so the heat is up, and the windows are closed. A middle-aged man in a flat top haircut is sitting behind the teacher's desk and reading the sports pages in the Asbury Park Press. His name is unimportant to the five high school students he is watching. The five students' names are equally unimportant to him. He glanced down at his ledger and just did a head count. They were given detention and were waiting for the last few minutes.

The first name on the ledger he only glanced at was Patricia Azzolini, an obese girl. She is sitting by the classroom windows and wiping away tears from her plump cheeks under her fogged-up glasses. Earlier in the day, Patricia was sitting in Spanish class when one of the more popular girls in school was sitting behind her decision to put gum in her hair. Patricia had enough and turned to slap the girl in the face. She missed it, but the teacher saw the swing and took Patricia out of class. Now with a clump of hair missing on the back of her head and two days of detention, Patricia sat sobbing.

The next name on the ledger was Alex Li. He was a freshman who had been printing out NCAA basketball brackets and taking bets from classmates. He was given a week's detention. He sat and did his homework two seats in front of Patricia.

By the door in the front of the class, and the third name on the ledger, was Kitty Elise. She was a junior who was caught smoking by the buses during lunch.

The fourth name on the ledger was Ron Putarski. He was a senior varsity football player who was given one day's detention for bullying a special needs student in gym class. During volleyball, Ron would spike the ball as hard as he could at the special needs student. The gym teacher caught on pretty quickly, and the detention was given out.

Michael Phy was the fifth and final name on the ledger, which was now being crumpled and thrown out. A junior who should have been a senior, he sat in the back of the class with a gray hooded sweatshirt on and his head down on the desk. He was in trouble for having incendiary materials in his locker - lighter fluid, a road flare, and greasy rags. A student with an adjoining locker saw what was inside and tipped off a janitor, who then relayed the information to the principal. He was given a week's detention pending further investigation. He most likely will face expulsion.

"Til' tomorrow." The unimportant detention monitor says.

The five students get up to leave. Michael has finally lifted his head off the desk. He has unkempt brown hair and brown eyes, almost black. The left eye is set lower than the right. He is thin with a strong jawline like his father, Paul.

Once outside the side exit of the school, Kitty lights up another cigarette. Alex puts on his headphones and listens to "Plush" by Stone Temple Pilots. Ron meets up with some jock friends and jumps in the back of a truck bed. Patricia has her head down, and books clutched to her chest. Michael has his hood on and walks past her. Up ahead by the school's front entrance, he sees two cop cars pull in. Michael stops and has a feeling they are there to question him. He turns and walks in the opposite direction to the back of the school building.

This would not be Michael's first run-in with the police. He had been caught before for a few minor infractions like trespassing, underage drinking, and petty theft from a convenience store, but nothing as serious as attempted arson. Michael can now see the back of the school grounds and the football field. Behind that were some woods he could cut through to get home. He gets to the football field entrance when he hears gravel crunching under car tires behind him. He knows the tires belong to the police cars. He turns to see them slowly pulling up next to him.

Michael is placed in the backseat without being cuffed. Officer James Gardener is giving him a ride home. James Gardener is the son of retired Toms River Police Officer Clarence Gardner. James is thirty-five years old and in his fourteenth year on the force.

"Michael, you have been expelled. The good news is the school won't press charges. They just want you gone. Can you stay gone, Michael?" Officer James Gardener asks while looking at him in the rearview mirror. Michael stays silent while looking out the car window.

"I'm guessing homelife isn't too good. I was shown your school file. Failing grades, antisocial behavior and prone to periodic violent episodes. Not too good. You're turning eighteen next month and will be tried as an adult if there are any further violations with us. Your story is going to go only two ways, Michael. The first way is to turn your life around and become a law-abiding citizen. The second way is you being behind bars or worse. My job is to make sure that you don't hurt anyone if you decide to choose the latter. Everything comes down to choices." James pulls the police cruiser to the front of the Phy house. He gets out of the car and opens the rear passenger door for Michael to get out. The two exchange glances and Michael walks to the front of the house. Michael doesn't turn back when he enters. James enters his squad car and looks back to the house before leaving.

While heading back to the precinct, James thinks of his town. He cares deeply for it. He has lived here in Toms River his whole life. James joined the academy directly out of college. He worked hard, paid his dues, and navigated through the precinct's double standards and systemic corruption to move up the ranks. Being the son of Clarence Gardener helped, but there were still pockets of racism in the precinct. In one year, he hopes to become a detective in the homicide division. After ten more years, he wants to take his talents to the Federal Bureau of Investigation. The only thing James married was his work - no wife, no children, only a nephew. He spent a lot of time with his eight-year-old nephew, Thomas. He was from his sister Denise who was divorced, but amicably. James felt Thomas could use a father figure, so he would take him fishing on Saturdays and to church on Sundays. The Gardener family were practicing Catholics even though James and Thomas were the only two in the family who regularly attended mass. James' mother passed away a few years earlier from breast cancer.

James would pray for his family, of course, and he would pray for his town. For the past few years, he has felt some foulness come over Toms River. A black cloud, an evil wind, he couldn't put his finger on it, but there was something amiss. Michael Phy worried him. The disfigured left eye and rap sheet before a driver's license made James uneasy. To James, Micheal Phy was the embodiment of a system failure and of bad things to come. Officer James Gardener was experienced and good at his job. He knew Michael was going to choose way number two.

Inside the kitchen, Michael stands by the open refrigerator. He takes one of his father's beers. He goes to the kitchen window and can see his father fumbling with an extracted car engine on a lift in the driveway. Michael has no desire to tell his parents he's been kicked out of school. He goes to the basement of the house. The basement is sort of a hangout Michael uses. He lays down on a cot and listens to "Rotten Apple" by Alice In Chains. He sips his beer. Michael's bedroom upstairs had been converted to a den after Laura left Paul ten years prior.

Michael visits his father from time to time but lives full-time with his mother in an apartment complex down by the east side of town. The separation was not amicable, but it was a long time coming. After Michael was born, Laura slipped into a long depression. For the first time in his life, Paul was not the center of attention, and he did not know how to handle that. There were arguments born from bitterness and resentment that they both secretly blamed on Michael. The fights were never physical, but Paul would make empty threats. After countless screaming matches and years of unhappiness, Laura, for her own sanity, decided to take Michael and leave. Paul kept the house and agreed to child support. The shame he felt from his family splintering has stayed with him. He began to examine himself and do some work to figure out why his family had left and how to become a better person. Paul realized his selfishness and need for control were problematic. The realization that controlling people only pushes them away allowed Paul to begin to let go.

In Emerald Apartment 6H, Laura has just gotten home from her morning shift at the grocery store. It is not the same family-owned grocery store she used to work as a teenager, but a larger, more corporate one. She is one of a hundred employees. After being up before dawn, Laura is exhausted and slumps down on the couch and lights a cigarette. She sifts through the junk mail on the coffee table while listening to the kids play in the adjoining apartment. Laura hates the apartment because it is too small with paper-thin walls. The furniture is all from thrift shops, and the wood floors are all scratched.

Laura sometimes misses the house she used to live in, but she does not miss Paul. She didn't fight for the house in court. She just wanted out but did not leave town because she wanted Michael to stay in the same school. Even in separation, Laura had to settle, and she did with this apartment. Explaining the separation to friends at work was difficult. Paul never abused Laura in the physical sense, he was not an alcoholic, and he was employed. The abuse was psychological, but time had healed some wounds. Laura did not hate Paul. She just was glad to be rid of him. Laura did not have difficulty explaining the separation to her mother. Helen was relieved and salvaged a relationship with her daughter before passing away ten months ago. A red blinking light from the answering machine in the living room catches Laura's eye. She gets up to play it. The message on the phone is from Michael's high school, notifying her that he has been expelled.

Paul is still in the driveway and has finally removed a seized piston. It took a blow torch, a wrench, and all of Paul's strength to get it out. He is exhausted and light-headed. He can gather himself and catch his breath at the workbench. Paul has had these episodes before, but now they last a little longer each time. He refuses to see a doctor for fear of the diagnosis. His father died of a heart attack, as did his grandfather. He knows he needs to lose weight and eat better, but he doesn't. It isn't so much the disease or the ailment that kills men. It is the stubbornness that does.

Paul makes his way to the backdoor of the house and enters the kitchen. He can overhear Michael talking on the telephone in the living room.

"I didn't do it. They called the cops and kicked me out." Michael says. "Ok, I'm coming home now." Michael hangs up the phone.

"What's going on?" Paul asks.

"I have to go. Mom is pissed because I got in trouble at school."

"What kind of trouble?"

Michael doesn't answer his father. He just grabs his backpack and heads out the front door. Paul is still too tired to chase after him and is left alone in the home he used to share with his family. Paul hoped to pass the family business on to Michael, but those hopes were quickly dashed when Michael's learning disabilities came to the forefront in adolescence. He tried to teach his son the basics of a bicycle once when Michael was eight. Michael just stared at him

blankly with his shoes untied. Paul realized Michael couldn't even tie his shoes. Paul became

disappointed, which led to him being disillusioned with his son. The two grew apart, and Paul

began to regret how he had raised him. Paul felt responsible for The problems Michael had in

school and life. He failed his son, and it tortured him.

The route to Emerald Apartments is a straight shot on Old Freehold Road. Michael is

walking and thinking of how angry his mother will be. Part of him wants to walk in the opposite

direction and never come back. He continues toward the apartment and has to walk past the high

school. He glares at it and moves on. His plan for the school was to see how big a fire he could

make before it was put out. Maybe even get school canceled for a day or two. Fire fascinated

him. The ease of making it and the amount of damage it could do excited him even aroused him.

To inflict a massive amount of destruction with little effort was what Michael desired. He just

had to figure out a way to do it. On the right, he walks past Riverside Cemetery. He can hear a

backhoe in the distance. Sometimes Michael would cut through the cemetery to get home. He

would see one of the workers there and recognize him from freshman year. The worker had

graduated two years ago and was one of the outcasts in school that Michael related to. He was

tall with long black hair and constantly in and out of the principal's office like Michael was.

When cutting through the cemetery, Michael would sometimes wave to him, and he would wave

back. Michael is in no rush to get home, so he continues on Old Freehold Road without seeing

Billy Mallek.

Riverside Cemetery is the oldest one in Toms River. It is the final resting place for three

thousand souls but has fallen into disrepair. Only two groundskeepers work to maintain the

multi-acre lot. A backhoe is digging a grave in the direct center of the property. A burial will happen tomorrow for a former New Jersey assemblyman. Operating the backhoe is Billy, now twenty years old. His long hair is pulled back into a ponytail, and his intimidating frame fills up the cab. Watching the hole being excavated is Freddy. He checks to see if the scoop on the backhoe doesn't crack open an adjacent grave. As the backhoe eats away more earth, Freddy watches Billy with pride. Freddy knows that Billy is a natural leader in the community and life. He is no-nonsense and intelligent. The last scoop of dirt is picked up and set on the side. The bucket lowers, and the engine cuts off. Billy and Freddy begin stabilizing the hole for the device that will lower the casket. Six ten-foot-long two-by-fours are placed around the hole. Two at the head and foot of the hole and four on each side. Then four ten-foot-long flat planks are placed on top of the left and right sides for the pallbearers to stand on with they place the casket on the lowering device. After the prep, Billy and Freddy take a break under a pine tree.

"Community barbecue on Saturday. Will you come? It would mean a lot if you did. The kids look up to you." Freddy wipes sweat off his brow.

"I'll drop by. How's mom?"

"She's fine. In fact, she's welcoming a new couple into the Community now. You should call her more."

"I would. It's just…"

"What?" Freddy asks.

"Her depression. That doesn't bother you?" Billy says, looking down at his worn, weathered and cracked boots. They remind him of his mother.

"She's taking her meds. She's coping. It's a temporary thing. Getting her out and involved more with the Community seems to help her mood. Is that why you don't call?" Asks Freddy.

"Yes. It can be too much sometimes."

"Calling might improve her mood, William."

Billy nods in agreement, goes back to the backhoe, and starts the engine. Freddy watches him, and like Billy, he worries about Angela's depression. Not once did Freddy think he was the cause of it. Billy takes the backhoe to the garage, and Freddy follows slowly behind on foot. As Freddy has gotten older, he feels himself getting weaker. Years of consuming animal and human blood have wreaked havoc on his body. He has contracted hepatitis and does his best to manage it. Freddy cannot control his appetite for blood, so he knows his days are few, which is why he needs a successor.

Sam Betancourt in New York is one possibility. Randy Claxton doesn't possess the leadership qualities that Freddy looks for, but Billy has the most promising future. Freddy hasn't told him all of the Community's secrets, but in time he will. Billy has been reluctant, which Freddy cannot understand. He knows Billy cares for the people of the Community, but he feels the petty crime and the ingesting of animal blood are beneath what they should be doing. The money was tempting to Billy, but taking portions of the elderly's social security and the young people's drug trafficking and prostitution felt unfair. Billy still, oddly enough, had his own moral code. He also knew it was only a matter of time until the Community got exposed. At least three times a day, a police cruiser would drive through Pine Acres. The police were sniffing, and eventually, they would find the meat.

Officer James Gardener is driving through Pine Acres while on patrol. He had discussions in the past with his father, Clarence, about this part of town. Clarence is very familiar with Pine Acres and its unorthodox proprietor Frederick Bile. He would tell James that if he had a map of that area of town, you would see crimes in all the surrounding areas except for Pine

Acres. James was fascinated by the rumors about the trailer park being filled with "blood drinkers" and "vampires." The fascination turned to frustration because they could operate and fund themselves by committing felonies all over town under the precinct's nose. They were well organized and rarely caught. They never would roll over on each other or Freddy Bile. He was smart, and his tenants were loyal. James knew he would need a miracle or an act of God to bring down Bile and his gang at Pine Acres. He sees Bile's girlfriend, Angela Mallek, showing a trailer to a young couple. James just shakes his head and drives out.

"They're called ghetto doctors?" Angela asks the young brunette with green eyes.

"They are real doctors and can get you whatever you ask for as long as you pay them upfront. The guy had a revolving door for addicts up in Newark. They are all over the state now." Alexis says.

Alexis Velai and her boyfriend Ricky Drayton are putting a down payment on a trailer. The two are from Newark and are recovering addicts. They have received government assistance and are looking for steady work and a home in the Toms River area. No other place would take them except for Pine Acres. Angela is showing them the outside. A wooden deer target and a rusted bicycle from the previous tenant are in the back. He was an elderly man that passed away two months prior from blood cancer. Ricky is a thin man in his late twenties and usually wears jeans, work boots, and a Peterbilt cap. He is staring at the deer target that is riddled with bullet holes. Angela leads them up the newly built wooden stairs to the front door. The inside of the trailer is empty and freshly painted. The windows are open to air out the cigarette smell from the previous occupant. Alexis and Ricky have no doubt they are taking this place, and Ricky puts his arm around his girlfriend.

"What do you think, babe?" Ricky asks.

"I think we'll take it." Alexis smiles.

"I guess all that's left is the paperwork. You sure you don't want to check another unit at the far end?" Angela asks.

"No, this is it. This is home." Alexis smiles at Angela.

While Angela is taking the young couple to the office, she thinks of being their age again. The years have been long for Angela. She is tired and withered in appearance, and her soul is aimless. When Alexis smiled at her, it was the first time in years that her heart had skipped a beat. Freddy never made her feel that way. The Community is what Freddy truly loved, and Angela was just along for the ride. Her relationship with Billy was strained. When he got to high school, he spent most of his time with friends, which wasn't unusual for a teenager. The problem was Angela and Freddy were not disciplinarians. Billy could be away for the whole night, and they would let him get away with it. Freddy would sometimes hand out a punishment, but that involved doing work around Pine Acres. When Billy was home, he was with Freddy and not her. She began to resent Freddy. Angela wanted to leave him, but she had little access to money and was afraid Freddy would have one of his goons rough her up and bring her back. She wasn't allowed to leave. One night in 1984 at Colgate Lake in upstate New York, Freddy had asked Angela to marry him. She turned him down because she was not in love with him. Freddy never looked at Angela the same way again.

Angela sat at her desk and watched as Alexis and Ricky signed the lease agreement. Angela noticed they both had matching rose tattoos. One on Ricky's left hand by the thumb and one on Alexis' right hand by her thumb. When the two held hands, the roses intertwined. Angela felt a twinge of jealousy.

Freddy is on his way back to the Community. He has just dropped off Billy at his girlfriend's place. On the way home, Freddy thought of Angela and her depression. He wanted her to get better, but he also took satisfaction in it. She suffered as he suffered when she turned down his proposal many years ago. Angela never loved Freddy, and Freddy knew it. Everything he did at the Community was done for selfish reasons and to impress Angela. Freddy wanted to show her that he was capable of grand ideas and following through on them. Despite his accomplishments, he was never able to make Angela love him. Freddy parks his truck and walks into the main office. He sees Angela with Alexis and Ricky. He smiles at the young couple without introducing himself. Before going to the back room, he noticed the young couple couldn't wipe the smiles from their faces. He also noticed that Angela couldn't take her eyes off the young woman.

Victoria Black has pale skin, black hair with purple streaks and tattoos up and down her arms and legs. She is smoking a cigarette while lying nude on her black satin sheets. She is listening to "Christian Woman" by Type O Negative. She was a senior in high school before dropping out three months ago. Her blue eyes match her boyfriend's. She first met him two years ago in the woods behind the school. She was smoking with a couple of her goth friends when he came to her and bummed a cigarette. She was immediately struck by his long black hair, blue eyes, and imposing physique. It was the first time she had felt that ache in her stomach for a boy. It was a pull that the sick have for medicine or a wolf to the moon. He was tall, dark, and mysterious. The pull got even stronger when she heard he was from "vampire village" on the west side of town. Curiosity is a natural aphrodisiac for a teenage girl, and Victoria had that for Billy Mallek.

Billy had taken Victoria to the Community, but only for brief periods. He didn't trust the other men there, especially Randy Claxton. Victoria was his, and he was very protective. The two were inseparable. She was intoxicated with his love. He was an outcast like she was. The truth about outcasts is that they want and crave acceptance. Billy was the first boy to accept her faults and all. She was also curious as to the reputation of the Community. After the trust was established, Billy admitted to her that he drank blood. Not human blood, but an animal. Instead of feeling repulsed, Victoria became aroused. During sex, she would make tiny cuts on her arms and legs for him to drink from. It became a ritual that cemented the love and trust between them. She loved feeding him. He loved feeding from her body. As Victoria lay in bed, she now began to ache for him. She began to feel the blood rush between her legs, and she wanted him. There was no need to deny her temptations. All she had to do was walk to the bedroom window, part the curtains and tap on the glass. Billy was outside in the backyard of her house. He was getting high with his friend Giovanni Gomez. Victoria got up and went to the window and parted the curtains. She taps on the glass, and Both Billy and Gio turn to see Victoria nude in the window. Billy gets up and comes inside while Victoria closes the curtains. Billy walks into the bedroom and walks to Victoria. He grabs her shoulders and pushes her down on the bed.

Giovanni Gomez is getting stoned while listening to the sex from the inside of the house while "Connection" by Elastica plays on the stereo. Gio had first met Billy in high school. They were the same age and would skip class together and hang out at the local convenience store. Gio came from a blue-collar Latino family. Both parents worked, and his sister was currently attending community college. Gio was a slacker. All he did was smoke weed, play video games, and sleep. Gio enjoyed rap music, but Billy had told him to listen to heavy metal, so he did. Billy was cool and intrigued the girls in school. Gio was a ghost until he met Billy. Billy was a leader, and Gio was a follower. Gio's father operated a junkyard and knew his way around cars. Billy used Gio's knowledge about car locks and bypassing their anti-theft devices to help him steal cars and parts for the Community's side business. With the little money Gio made from stealing car parts and selling weed to friends, he would go to the local strip club "Delilah's" on Route 9. He was carded every time, but he was over eighteen, and the club didn't serve alcohol. Billy never went because he felt those places degraded women. Part of that was because his mother was a dancer for a brief period. Gio loved the illusion of the club. Gorgeous girls giving him attention. He could practice pick-up lines, sometimes in Spanish, and try to score phone numbers he never got. Now, most days were spent hanging out at Victoria's house. Gio's parents were disappointed in their son's aimless direction in life. He was a dropout and was never home. The few times he was home, he would sleep most of the day away. He felt his parent's disappointment, which only increased his anxiety and guilt. The weed and alcohol helped mask the depression, and Billy helped Gio feel that at least someone cared. Gio would do anything for Billy, even kill.

After sex, Billy had gone to the bathroom. Victoria was completely spent and enjoying the comedown. She was intoxicated, infatuated, devoted and totally in love. She, too, had come under the spell of Billy. A series of bad choices and dark roads at a young age led her to him. Victoria began smoking at twelve, drinking at thirteen, and taking drugs by fifteen. She dabbled in cutting herself. She did it to get her mother's attention or anyone's attention. Her father left when she was young, and her mother worked multiple jobs to pay the rent in their current house. Music was her escape; she changed her hair and modified her body with ink and piercings. No one noticed until Billy. When he asked her for the cigarette behind the school, he noticed the old scars on her arms and wrists. He knew she suffered somehow and enjoyed the sight of her own blood. Billy had zeroed in on Victoria and knew she would be his.

Billy needed blood to feel nourished. He was tired of pig, chicken and fish blood. He wanted to try human blood, and if he could reopen those scars on Victoria's arms, it would satiate him. It might even give Victoria the sense of belonging that she desperately needed. Not just a blood donor but his very own concubine. Victoria was now in bed, lightly touching her old scars and new cuts on her arms and legs. They were not cut out of pain or a cry for attention but with a purpose. She was feeding her man. She was doing something unique, taboo, and empowering. Infrequently, Billy would also cut himself just under his pectoral and let Victoria feed from him. He saw this in the film "Bram Stoker's Dracula," and it was something he wanted to do with the woman he loved. Victoria was indifferent to the taste, but for Billy, she would indulge. Victoria never thought of the past anymore. Her love for Billy had freed that burden. Only the future lay ahead, which revolved around her and her boyfriend.

Freddy sat at the dining room table, watching Angela in the kitchen. She was staring out the window towards the trailer Alexis and Ricky had just rented. Freddy knows of her depression and that she possibly wanted out of the Community. Angela never wanted to know the intimate details of the underground networking there, and she wanted to know even less about the blood rituals. Angela handled the books, and that was all. The Happy Hour had closed five years prior and was bulldozed. Now in its place was a two-story dental office. He knows she became bored after losing some of the independence her bartending job afforded her. Freddy also knows she may have taken a liking to the pretty young tenant across the way.

"No dinner?" He asks.

"Hamburgers. Medium rare. Coming up." Angela says, snapping out of her fog.

"How do you like the new people? Alexis and Richard?" Freddy said, never taking his eyes off Angela.

"They seem fine. You know how young couples are. Just looking for a fresh start."

"Good. They will get that here. That Alexis girl had a resemblance to you when you were that age. Are they getting married?" Freddy wonders.

"I think so. They're just young. Blind devotion to each other. Naive in a way."

"Devotion to one another is a good thing. We can benefit from that. They may have that devotion to other things if they have that capacity. Do they have employment?"

"Ricky was a welder, and Alexis hasn't found anything yet. She is a little worried about that." Angela says, knowing Freddy is digging for something.

Freddy's mind begins to churn. Freddy likes to find one weak spot in a person to exploit for his own gain. He did it to get Angela. He did it to get Pine Acres. Now he wants to do it again to get Alexis. It has been months since the Community had a donor, and plenty of empty storage containers were buried in the woods behind the property. Much like the long-deceased Rebecca Bailey, Alexis needed money. Freddy is an off-the-books owner of Charlie's Bar, one mile down the road. A dive bar is mostly only frequented by biker gangs or truckers driving through town.

"Charlie needs a bartender. Ask her if she wants to pick up a shift."

"That place is a dump. A little dangerous for a young girl."

"She needs money. Nobody will give her trouble. Ask her." The tone Freddy has insinuates to Angela that he isn't asking.

"I'll tell her. What about Ricky? He needs work." The hamburgers begin to sizzle on the stove, so Angela shuts off the flame.

"He'll have to find that on his own."

Angela brings over two hamburgers to the table. One for her and one for Freddy. Angela's is done medium well.

"Ricky might not like her working at Charlie's. Could cause a problem."

"Like any young man, he will do what the girl wants," Freddy says.

Angela nibbles on her food, and her mind drifts to Billy being distant, Freddy being controlling, Alexis being beautiful, Tasha being gone and her insignificance.

Chapter 17

April, 1998

Paul is in the backyard raking up some remaining winter leaves from around the deck. As he nears retirement, Paul finds it difficult to find things to keep himself occupied. One project he has in mind is to rebuild this very deck. The paint has long since faded, and holes have appeared on top, making it dangerous. The support beams underneath are rotting, and clumps of black and wet leaves are caked around them. Paul pulls out the clumps by hand and sees an old wasp nest. He recalls Michael being stung by a wasp as a boy and how much he cried. Paul has only been doing yard work for fifteen minutes and is tired. He sits on the first step of the desk and closes his eyes. He can hear the wind in the trees and the street traffic out front. He can hear birds chirping and a dog barking four houses down. He can also hear his heart pounding in his chest.

Laura is taking a smoke break on the side of the grocery store. She watches families enter and leave the parking lot. She is keen to watch single mothers with young children and takes a small bit of happiness because those days are over. The work was overwhelming. Michael wasn't hyper or difficult to control when he was younger. He was very quiet but required a lot of attention. He never brushed his hair or teeth on his own and couldn't dress himself until he was ten. When Laura did take him with her food shopping, he would sit in the child seat in the front of the carriage as a toddler. His head would be down, and he would only look up and show excitement when they got to the store cereal aisle. He liked all the colorful characters and lettering on the boxes. He would always point to the boxes that had a small plastic toy inside.

Laura never bought him those cereals. She always bought generic knockoff brands with black and white lettering and no toy. Subconsciously Laura didn't buy him those cereals to teach him a lesson. The lesson is that you can't always get what you want. Laura didn't. She wanted a girl but instead got a boy with a slightly disfigured face. Her face was on him but askew. Laura always focused on Michael's right eye when talking to him because the sagging left eye disgusted her. She cared for him, clothed him, fed him, and washed him, but she never loved him.

Most parents will treat a child as a blessing, but Laura and Paul treat their child like an obligation. There were no fond memories, no family vacations, no parent-teacher conferences, no birthday celebrations, and no graduation ceremony. There was no nurturing, encouraging, or listening. Laura and Paul did the bare minimum with Michael, and only now did it set in. Putting out her cigarette and watching the single mothers come in and out of the grocery store, Laura has a bit of remorse. She takes a moment before returning to work and wishes she had bought him the cereal with the toy inside.

The windows in James Gardener's police cruiser are down as he drives over the Tunney Bridge from Seaside Heights into Toms River. He hopes to smell the salt water from Barnegat Bay below, but he can't. He can't remember the last time he had. Summer is only two months away, and the air is still cold. Spring is not as warm as he remembers it being when he was growing up. James knows something is foul and wrong in his town. He has felt this way for a few years, especially when he is at a crime scene or in the aftermath of a deadly traffic accident. Evil has crept into his town. It's in the odorless saltwater, the cold wind, and the people. James would sometimes confess his feelings to fellow officers and family members, but they would shrug it off, saying he had just been on the job too long and needed time off. James knew better, and so did his father.

"There are bad people out there in the world, James. When you take this job, you will come face to face with them, and when you do, you better act first." Clarence told James once while on a fishing trip. Those words have stayed with James ever since. The only time James feels safe is at church on Sunday afternoon mass. He takes his young nephew Thomas with him. His sister Denise's only child. Denise and her ex-husband Jason work on Sundays, so James watches Thomas on Sundays. In the morning, they go fishing, and it's Catholic mass at five in the afternoon. Most black families in Toms River are Baptist, but Clarence Gardener was able to afford the tuition to send his children to Catholic school. The routine of the mass gave James a sense of normalcy. The praying, singing, listening, and giving to the church gave James a glimmer of hope and the strength to push on for another week. Once outside the church, however, James could feel the weight of the sky's black clouds and the Devil's wicked snares just beyond his vision. Toms River had its problems that cities much larger had. Drugs, prostitution, gangs, shootings, robberies, vandalism, child abuse and animal cruelty. The children and the animals bothered James the most. The innocent are the most vulnerable.

Certain pockets of town gave James a sense of pause. Route 166 and Route 37 had an intersection that had seen multiple accidents. The Pine Acres trailer park on the west side of town, with its "vampire village" moniker, bothered him. Riverside Cemetery began to bother him, especially when he would see Frederick Bile there. Not far from the cemetery was Toms River High School North, which for reasons unknown to James, started giving him a sense of foreboding when he drove past. The brick structure stood on the corner of Old Freehold Road and looked like any normal suburban high school. It was quiet. Too quiet. James circled the school twice and couldn't put his finger on what was bothering him. He pulled away and headed toward the police station. All the while, he thought of getting back to church on Sunday.

After his expulsion, his parents forced Michael to find gainful employment. The last week in April, he secured a part-time job as a power washer for a local landscaping company. He found the job in the free classified circulars in front of a grocery store. The training lasted all of a day, but the work was steady. Michael was given a call every morning during the week to either wash off aluminum siding on a home, a moss-covered driveway, a sidewalk, mud-caked decks, and patios. The work was easy, and his boss gave him a 1985 Dodge Ram to take from job to job. The power washing unit and hoses were kept in the truck bed. The brakes squealed, the wipers didn't work, and the headlights were long burnt out. Michael is indifferent to the work. He does enjoy it when the water pellets bounce off a home's siding. The spray blows back into his face and keeps him cool off. The constant noise of the power washer engine puts Michael in a trance. His mind drifts to when things began going wrong for him. The truth was since birth, but for Michael, the moment that sticks out is when he broke into the high school one night in his freshman year two years ago.

In shop class during his freshman year, Michael had been making a wooden candlestick holder and was almost finished. The only problem was that one inch in diameter copper fitting that holds the candle wouldn't sit in the circular groove. Michael took out a small pocket knife to level off the circular groove. The blade was three inches long and serrated. When the shop teacher saw Michael take out a knife, he immediately confiscated it. Michael tried to plead his case that it was just for shop class and a present from his father, but the principal didn't care and told Michael it would be mailed to him at the end of the school year. It was not to be brought in anymore. Michael was lying. The knife was for self-defense and was not given to him by his father. A senior gave the knife to him earlier in his freshman year. Michael was in the school bathroom with toilet paper shoved into his nostrils to stop bleeding from a broken nose. Kids had been calling him "Sloth" during lunch, and Michael took a swing at one but missed and was jumped by two members of the junior varsity football team.

"Why Sloth?" The senior asks.

"From 'The Goonies.' His eyes were crooked."

"You don't look like Sloth. If they come at you again, you just give them a surprise." The senior reaches into his back pocket and takes out the knife. He gives it to Michael.

"I'm not going to stab anyone."

"You won't have to. Once they see it, they'll run off. Just make sure no one sees you with it, and you didn't get that from me." The bell rings, and before the senior leaves, he says, "Good luck."

"Thanks," Michael says while playing with the knife, opening and closing it. He then replaces the blood-soaked toilet paper in his nose. He looks at himself in the cracked bathroom mirror. This was the first time Michael had met the senior Billy Mallek.

Now the knife was stuck in a drawer in one of the many rows of green metal filing cabinets in a long hallway in the school's main office. The hallway connected the front office administration to the principal's office. Michael wanted it back, so he decided to break in at night and take it. The school's laundry room had many large windows left open at night to vent out the steam from the dryers. The linens and uniforms for the scholastic sports teams were washed daily, and the upper windows were left open, especially in warmer months. The laundry room was located in the back of the school. Michael crept around and hid in the trees behind the school. He waited for the security car to pass by, and when it did, he dashed for the back windows. The windows were high but not impossible to get into. Michael had propped himself up on the brick window sill and pulled himself up and in the top window. It was dark, and the ten washers and dryers were all on and making a lot of noise. Michael simply walked through the dimly lit halls and was conscious of any noise his footsteps made. The door to the front office was open, and Michael stayed low until he got to the metal filing cabinets. In the distance, he could hear a janitor waxing the floors with a buffer machine, so Michael wanted to be quick. The cabinets were in alphabetical order, and he rushed to the N-O-P drawer. He found his manilla folder. "Phy, Michael F-166." The "F" was for freshmen. The folder was heavy, and sure enough, inside a plastic bag was the pocketknife. He took it and replaced it with a kitchen butter knife he had stolen from home. He was ready to bolt out of a front classroom window across the hall, but curiosity had gotten the best of him. He began reading his file. Various school infractions from elementary and middle school were listed. Standardized test scores, including the IOWA test score. Nothing was all that interesting until he saw a paper with the heading "Psyche and Mental Health Report." The report had been based on, but not limited to, teacher reports, absences and tardiness, guidance counselor reports, doctor notes and health recommendations, all kept since kindergarten. A sort of tertiary psychological profile had been developed by a doctor Michael had never met. Dr. Sandra Mehtze of The Children's Psychiatric Hospital of Hackensack drew up the report of Michael Anthony Phy. Certain phrases and sentences caught his attention. "Imbecilic effort with little comprehension of standard criteria." As well as "antisocial tendencies, delinquency and apparent lack of self-control or awareness put the subject in a high-risk category. Not out of the realm of possibility that the subject, who exhibits borderline personality characteristics, could do harm to himself and others. Quarterly visits with a school psychologist are recommended." Michael closes the file and puts it back in the cabinet. He is covered in sweat from the anger and betrayal he feels. The cold terminology, information collected, and assumptions made cut through him. He doesn't remember how he got out of school that night two years ago. All he remembers is the long walk home with his knife back in his pocket and a rage he had never felt before.

As he loads the power washer into the back of his work truck, a small portion of those terrible feelings resurface. To be categorized and labeled without anyone knowing you are hurtful. You cease being an individual and become words on a page in a file in a green metal cabinet. The desire to watch his school burn down to the ground started that night. Nothing left except twisted metal and ash. His record was lost forever. He remembers the following day, after the break-in, how he stole a one-gallon metal container of gasoline from his father's garage and some greasy rags. He remembers going to Winding River Park at dusk and finding a secluded wooded area only accessible by foot. He experimented with gasoline and rags, building a fire as big as possible. Branches and dried long grass were tossed into it, and the flames reached as high as his head. It gave Michael relief to feel the fire's heat on his face. The tension eased, and the inklings of therapy for him began to emerge. Destroying makes things better. It gave him power and control, which he had never experienced before.

As he drives his work truck home, he smiles fondly, remembering the revelation fire had given him. He passes by St. Joseph's Church near downtown Toms River. Religion had interested Michael, but never enough to learn about it or practice it. Laura and Paul never took him to church and never spoke of God to him. All Michael had learned about religion was from television and movies. He knew of Jesus, the Crucifixion, Satan, Heaven, Hell, and the Apocalypse. While stopped at a red light by the church, Michael decided that he wanted to learn more. The best way to learn would be to read the Bible. Tomorrow he wants to go inside the church and steal one.

As Michael is on his way to drop off the work truck at his boss' home, Paul is driving through Island Heights. Today he feels like revisiting some of his old favorite spots around town. Island Heights was where he took Laura on their first date. Not much has changed except that the wooden planks of the boardwalk have been replaced a few times due to wear and tear. He watches people jog, senior citizens walk, and children ride bikes. His son, Michael, never learned to ride a bike. He would always fall over or hit a bush or tree and get discouraged. It wasn't as if Paul or Laura tried very hard to get him to keep trying. Before Island Heights, Paul had visited the street where the Happy Hour used to be. It was shut down due to financial hardships, and a bad reputation for bar fights and accidents as a more unruly clientele seeped in. Most of them were from the west side of town where Freddy lived. Paul hasn't had much contact with Freddy or Angela in recent years. Once in a while, they would bump into each other at the supermarket or the fireworks on the bay downtown. Paul had heard the rumors about Pine Acres but didn't believe them. Paul leaves Island Heights and drives past Brooks Road, where the film "The Amityville Horror" was shot. The infamous story occurred in Long Island but was filmed in Toms River. Paul remembers seeing camera crews back then.

Time passed quickly, and the good memories of himself and Laura began to fade. He cannot believe Laura left him, and he regrets the mess that Michael has become. Through soul searching over the last couple of years, Paul finally admitted that he shoulders some of the blame for what happened to his family. He never married Laura out of laziness and procrastination. She resented him for that, and he knew it. He let Laura raise their son and kept his distance when he saw how bad Michael's afflictions were. He would rather drink than invest. He failed his son, and that cuts deepest of all. His heart hurts as he drives home. It also hurts for medical reasons.

St. Joseph's Church on Hooper Avenue was rebuilt in 1993 to accommodate a larger occupancy. It is the newest, most expensive, and most aesthetically pleasing of all the churches in town. Adjacent to it are the Catholic High School and elementary school. The buildings share two large parking areas. This is where Michael parks his work truck this morning. He has a power washing job in fifteen minutes, so if he wants this Bible, he knows to get it fast. The church is empty on a weekday morning. The early morning mass ended a half hour ago. Michael walks into the church, through the lobby slash entryway and into the church's nave, where masses are held. He passes a dozen or so pews and looks up at the ten-foot wooden interpretation of the crucifixion of Christ. Michael doesn't have any religious background, so he has no understanding of the sacrifice made by God, allowing his son to be killed for the forgiveness of our sins. A chance is given to us by Christ to believe. Michael stares at the cross blankly and tilts his head to one side, trying to understand the enduring image. He is running out of time, so he looks around at the altar.

No one is inside, so he does a quick once over and sees no Bible. The pews have psalm books, but even Michael knows a Bible should be much thicker. He exits the main area of the church and walks around the lobby that encircles the church. There is a door, "Priest's Quarters," ahead, but it is locked. Inside are copies of the Bible, the gospel, priestly robes and garments. This is where the priest practices his homily after the gospel is read. It's a sort of explanation of the teachings in the gospel so the congregation can get a better understanding. Michael is at a loss and can hear voices getting louder down the lobby hall. He quickly exits the church through a side door.

The first house on Magnolia Lane in downtown Toms River belongs to Mrs. Ruth Weltzer, a seventy-five-year-old widow living alone in a ranch-style home. Michael's work truck is parked out front, and Michael is in the backyard hooking up the garden hose to the power washer. Mrs. Weltzer is talking to him through an open screen door.

"Three hours, you said, for the whole house?" She asks.

"Yes, I'll try to be quicker if you need it."

"No, that should be fine. I'll keep the door open if you need the bathroom. I'll leave the check here by the couch. Just let me know when you're finished." Mrs. Weltzer says.

Michael is surprised to hear how trusting she is. They have never met, and she unlocks her home to a total stranger. It isn't like Michael will do something. It's just the naivety she has. She leaves to go inside the home, and Michael walks to the screen door to look inside to see where she placed the check. It sits on a coffee table, and a bookshelf is across the couch and table. A thick, white, fake leather book catches his attention. The book's spine is gold and says, "Holy Bible." Michael will not take it now. He will simply wait until the power washing job is completed, and before he takes the check, he will simply enter the home, take it and put it under the driver's seat of his truck. Mrs. Weltzer reads a second Bible in her bedroom when her faith wavers. The Bible in the living room was a gift from her daughter that was never opened. It is not until the following Christmas, when her daughter visits, that she discovers it missing.

Laura is sitting at the kitchen table in the apartment, clipping coupons. She is aware that Michael has gotten home and, from the corner of her eye, sees him go past the kitchen towards his bedroom. She did not see the thick book he was carrying under his right arm. Words are seldom exchanged between mother and son, only brief acknowledgments. Michael's room is cluttered with video games, compact discs, clothes and walls adorned with posters of heavy metal bands. He slumps down on his bed and begins to read the Bible. He opens to a random passage. The vision in his right eye is near perfect, but the vision in his sagging left eye is compromised and makes the words appear blurry. He pushes through and reads "Thessalonians

2: 3-4. Let no one deceive you in any way. For the day will not come unless the rebellion comes first. The man of lawlessness is revealed, the son of destruction who opposes and exalts himself against every so-called god or object of worship so that he takes his seat in the temple of God, proclaiming himself to be God." Not having a religious education, Michael takes a yellow highlighter, scars the book by highlighting this passage, and continues reading and unknowingly defacing his stolen Bible.

Chapter 18

April, 1998

Same Day

Further west of town at Pine Acres, Angela shares a cigarette with Alexis on the front steps of Angela and Freddy's trailer.

"Ricky at work?"

"Yeah, I start tomorrow at Charlie's Bar. First work I've had in over a year. Hope he's not an asshole." Alexis says, taking a long drag.

"He's okay. If he gives you any shit, just tell me. He won't mess with any friend of Freddy's. It's good you're making your own money. Independence is important." Angela says, taking the cigarette.

"Ricky won't ever leave me. Not, after all we've been through. He's the one." Alexis says. She extends her hand to touch Angela's hand. "I want to thank you for being such a good friend to me, Angie. Everyone here has been so nice." Angela's heart skips a beat at the touch of her hand. She looks into Alexis' eyes and feels a connection.

"Come with me," Alexis says. She takes Angela's hand and leads her to her and Ricky's trailer across the tiny street. The inside of the trailer is still filled with moving boxes, and some knick-knacks are placed neatly on tables. Candle holders, snow globes, and tiny porcelain clowns were given to Alexis by her grandmother years ago.

"It needs work, I know, but the bedroom is all unpacked. You can take a look if you want.

Do you drink coffee?" Alexis asks.

"I do." Angela moves down the hall to the bedroom and sees the bed with a purple comforter on top with incense burning on a night table. She imagines making love to Alexis. She thinks of her kiss and how new and intoxicating it would be. Still, the thought quickly vanishes when she hears the coffee pots and cupboards moving around in the kitchen.

"I've never been good in the kitchen," Alexis says.

"Me neither, but you will get the hang of it when you have kids." Angela is now sitting at the kitchen table.

"Have you always lived here?"

"No, I was a Philly girl. Moved here with my son a long time ago. He doesn't talk to me much anymore."

"Why not?" Alexis asks.

"Things didn't turn out like they should have. I think he blames me for that."

"You loved him. He had a home. What more could you really do?"

Alexis sits across from Angela at the table. Her foot accidentally brushes against Angela's leg, making Angela's heart flutter.

"Sorry, cramped in here. Coffee will be ready in a couple minutes."

"Our place isn't much bigger. I'm guessing you and Ricky will save up for a home." Angela asks. She is a little flushed from the unintentional contact under the table.

"Won't be for years. It's okay as long as you're with people you love. Anywhere can be a home if you have that."

"I guess this place never really felt like home to my son."

"Maybe when he gets older, he will appreciate what you did for him."

Angela notices two coffee mugs on the kitchen counter. The two have pictures of roses, similar to the tattoos Alexis and Ricky share on their hands. Alexis gets up from the table and pours the coffee for them. She sits back down at the table.

"Thank you. Nice to be meeting normal people for a change." Angela says. She takes a sip of her coffee, which tastes sour, but she doesn't want to hurt Alexis' feelings, so she says nothing. A long look is shared as the two lock eyes.

"Everyone here seems normal. It is nice to make new friends." Alexis is making a subtle attempt to define her and Angela's relationship. This is not the first time a woman has taken an interest in her, and she is familiar with the longing in Angela's eyes. She is flattered, but she is very much in love with Ricky.

Later that night, Angela is now home and lying on the couch. She thinks of Alexis. She knows Freddy has plans for her and Ricky to stay and work for the Community, but she is not sure in what capacity. Angela is not naive to what the Community is and how it earns money. She doesn't want Alexis to fall into the same traps other young people have been caught up in when they move in. Angela thinks of Rebecca Bailey, who left the Community eleven years ago to go back home up north. Rebecca had promised to stay in touch but never did make a phone call or write a letter. Angela had her suspicions. *Had Freddy killed her?* The thought made her blood run cold. Alexis will not suffer the same mysterious fate as Rebecca and the dozen young women who have come through the Community over the years. Angela will not let Freddy corrupt or do worse to Alexis. If it came down to it, Angela would tell Alexis to leave Pine Acres even if it meant Angela would face the consequences in the process. The Community and Freddy had to be stopped. The question was how. Angela sits down at the desk and begins to write a letter.

Freddy walks up the three wooden steps to the trailer's front door and stops himself to grab hold of the guardrail. He hasn't feasted on blood or any other member of the Community in months. Animal blood wasn't sufficient enough to keep the feeders satiated. This was all in their minds, and their minds were easily corrupted by their own delusions. Of course, they didn't need blood to stay alive. They convinced themselves that any fatigue, soreness, or illness could be cured by ingesting blood. Freddy was sick with hepatitis, a result of drinking blood. He fooled himself into thinking he must have fresh, healthy blood to counteract the symptoms he was experiencing. He just needed secrets on Alexis to exploit, and Angela hopefully got some information. Freddy goes inside and sees Angela on the couch lying down

"Did you talk to our new tenant today?" Freddy asks.

"I did." Angela doesn't bother getting up. She stares at the water-stained ceiling.

"And?"

"Not much to say. She's happy to be here. She's looking forward to working tomorrow. I get the feeling she might want a family one day." Angela is careful not to divulge any personal information to Freddy. She will drag this out until she finds a way to save Alexis. Ricky was just a throw-in.

"That's not good enough. I need to know more."

"Why? So you can turn her out in the streets? Or worse?"

"We need to earn. I know this part of the business makes you uncomfortable, and that's why I shield you from it. I do need it. However, information and her wanting a family isn't good enough." Freddy says while watching Angela on the couch. He's looking for tells that she's lying. A twitch, a cough, or labored breathing. He's gotten good at spotting a lie over the years.

"Okay, Freddy. I'll keep digging."

"Good." Freddy walks to the bathroom.

Angela gets up from the sofa, looks out the living room window, and watches Alexis and Ricky's trailer. Freddy is lightheaded and washing his face in the bathroom sink. His worsening illness has put him in a very weak state, but that's not what truly bothers him. He noticed Angela never making eye contact with him. He knows she is lying.

While Freddy dreams of a nude woman with blonde hair and no face being burned at the stake, Angela creeps out of the trailer and walks quietly to Alexis and Ricky's trailer. She can see a light on through a slit in the living room curtains. The grass is wet, the air is cool, and Angela hopes Alexis is awake. She gets to the window and peeks in to see Alexis watching television herself on the couch. Angela walks around the side and up the steps quietly but quickly. She taps on the cheap metal door. Alexis ignores the first round of tapping, thinking it is just a cat. The second round of tapping gets her attention, and she goes to the door and looks out the peephole. She sees Angela looking nervously over her shoulders, so Alexis lets her in.

"What's going on, Angie?"

"We need to talk. Is Ricky asleep?" Angela asks quietly.

"Yes. Are you okay?"

"I know this is a bad time, but it's important. Let's sit." Angela sits with Alexis on the couch. She takes Alexis' hands.

"This place isn't what you think it is. Freddy is not who you think he is. They call it a Community. It's a cult."

"A cult? Devil worshippers?" Alexis asks with a tremble in her voice.

"Blood drinkers. Freddy finds people to move here who are young and vulnerable. He gets them to work for him. They do things that are illegal to pay for this place. It's a closed-off, tight-knit commune of criminals who drink…..blood.”

“Vampires? We moved next to a bunch of blood-drinking vampires?” Alexis asks while taking her hands away from Angela’s grasp.

“You have to leave. You and Ricky leave tonight.”

“Or what? He’ll kill us?”

“I don’t know. I do know that people have ended up missing.”

“Jesus Christ.” “Why are you telling me this?” Alexis gets up from the couch and begins pacing.

“It has to end. I don’t want anything to happen to you.” Angela stands and goes to the door. “I have to get back. Leave tonight or tomorrow if you can.”

“Just go. Please, just go.”

A lump forms in Angela’s throat as she turns the doorknob to exit.

“I’m sorry.” Angela leaves.

Alexis is at a loss. She doesn’t know what to do or say to Ricky. The story is so far-fetched that he won’t believe it and won’t want to leave. She goes to the curtains and watches Angela go back to her trailer. She begins biting her nails. *What if they break in tonight and kill us?* The thought sends her heart pumping. The best thing to do is to wake up Ricky and tell him that she just heard word for word from Angela. That is exactly what she does.

Angela is back at her trailer and closes the door behind her. She slides down the door and slumps on the floor. She is heartbroken about telling Alexis to leave, but she is also relieved to have told the truth. The thought of Alexis getting out of this place is good enough, even if it means Angela stays in the Community with her life hanging on by a thread. She knows Freddy’s reaction will not be good when he sees Alexis and Ricky are gone. Angela gets up off the floor and gingerly tip-toes to the bedroom. She sees Freddy on the side of the bed with covers over him. She pops off her slippers and slips into bed. She exhales and is relieved Freddy is not awake.

Freddy has been awake the whole time. He watched Angela leave the trailer and walk to the new tenant's trailer. He saw her enter and stay for five minutes and leave. He went back to bed and pretended to be asleep. His fury has his heart pounding, and his mind is getting cloudy as it fills with ways to force the truth from Angela. He placed a phone call to Randy while she was gone. Randy was instructed to park his truck behind Freddy's trailer with the engine off. Freddy and Randy will take Angela somewhere and find out what she told the new and ruined tenants. *Perhaps she told them nothing, but the risk was too great.* Freddy had worked too hard to have a rat inside the Community destroy his vision. Alexis and Ricky will be dealt with after he figures out what they know from Angela. He has not been this upset with her since she rejected his proposal years ago. In his heart, he knew she was never in love with him. She never looked at him the same way she did Tasha Higgins or the same way she would look at Alexis Velai. When Freddy hears rustling and doors slamming from a trailer across the way, he finally has the proof he dreaded. Alexis and Ricky are leaving in the dead of night. There's nothing he can do about them now. What he can do now is deal with Angela. Angela also hears the rustling across the way and panic sets in. *They're making too much noise. Freddy wakes up, and...* Freddy sits up in bed and turns towards Angela.

"You told them." Freddy's words are the last thing that Angela remembers.

At around four in the morning, Freddy is pacing in the dark living room. One sack of clothes is packed by the front door. *She gave me no other choice. People will ask too many questions and call the police. They will come and look for her. William will think the worst.*

Betancourt should be closed now. They can not find her. The thoughts are continuously in Freddy's head as he tries to focus. There is a light knock on the front door. Freddy opens the door to see a disheveled Randy.

"It's done," Randy says, almost out of breath.

"Samuel is on his way. I will be out of communication for a while. William will try to come to New York. Follow him. When he's close, you are to call me and not engage. He will be after me. I alone will deal with him."

"What if he doesn't understand? She may have destroyed this place for good. You had no choice." Randy says.

"Despite everything, she is still his mother. He will believe I killed her and want vengeance. He's smart, so keep vigilant." Freddy says as he hears a truck pull up to the front of his trailer. Sam Betancourt has come down from the second Community in New York to collect Freddy. Randy was the initial call, and the second call was to Sam. Sam enters the trailer.

"Are we ready? Sun will be up soon." Sam says. Freddy turns to Randy one last time.

"Say nothing to the police. Say nothing about New York. If members want to leave, then let them. This is self-preservation until I get things sorted." Freddy grabs his sack of clothes and leads the two men out of his trailer. Randy goes to his truck, and Freddy goes with Sam to his truck. The engines start, but the headlights are off. The trucks go in opposite directions. Some members of the Community have watched carefully and sheepishly through parted curtains and worry. They know something bad has happened and wonder if the Community's days are over.

The question of how to bring down the Community was familiar. It was the same way Roy "Priest" Higgins was brought down. A letter. In fact, two letters were written by Angela and put in the mailbox the night she disappeared. The first was to the Toms River Police Department detailing what she knew of the illegal activities at Pine Acres Mobile Park. The second letter was sent to the home of Billy's girlfriend. Victoria handed the letter to Billy when it arrived two days later. The note Angela had written said she loved him with all her heart and was apologetic about her choices. The biggest regret was Freddy and living at Pine Acres. The letter also said that if she ever went missing, the Community killed her. Billy and Victoria drove to Pine Acres that afternoon. The two went to Angela and Freddy's trailer. There was no answer when they knocked on the door. Billy peeked in through the windows and saw nothing unusual.

"There's no one here."

"What do you want to do, baby?" Victoria asks.

"Randy's trailer."

The two walk through the small streets of Pine Acres to the back west lot of Randy Claxton. It used to belong to his mother until she died three years prior. Randy's truck is not anywhere in sight. Billy walks to the front door and knocks. Nothing.

"There's always someone here. They might be in New York."

"Then let's go. Do you think they really killed her? We should bring Gio."

Billy notices the curtains opening and closing in the adjacent trailers. He can see the elders of the Community sitting on their front porches, watching him and Victoria. The two walk back to Victoria's car and leave Pine Acres. As they exit, four police cruisers enter with lights flashing.

It is dusk, and Victoria is driving while Billy is in the passenger seat, lost in his thoughts. Gio is asleep in the backseat. They are heading north on the Garden State Parkway. The sky is turning purple, and the traffic is still heavy, even at the end of rush hour. Billy is torn. Yes, he had a falling out with his mother for reasons she could and could not control, but she was still the only real blood relative he had. Billy was loyal to Freddy. He had raised him since he was an infant. He was the closest thing to a father he had known. Freddy was a mentor and a monster. Billy knew of the Community and all of its corruption. He also knows of the young women who went missing. Billy had his theories but never told Freddy of his misgivings and suspicions. The three men that ran the Community were Freddy, Sam, and Randy.

Freddy and Randy were missing, so it made sense to Billy that they simply headed north to the second Community in upstate New York. Billy wanted to confront Freddy and get answers. He needed them. The letter his mother wrote ate at him. She is missing, and she might be dead. Billy could have never imagined killing Freddy until he saw Randy's truck following them in the passenger side mirror. At that moment, Billy knew he was in danger. Randy had been trying to keep his distance, but his pickup truck had half an exhaust and had a noticeable sound that Billy picked up on. The heavy rumble of the exhaust roused him, and he glanced at his mirror, and sure enough, there was Randy.

"We're being followed."

"By who? Cops?" Victoria asks.

"Randy. Don't check the mirror. Just drive." Billy says, straightening himself up.

"What do we do?" She asks nervously.

"When we cross the state line, we'll pull over for gas. We have to lose him. Freddy always has a plan." They continue into the early hours of the evening with the faint skyline of New York City on the right and an uncertain night ahead.

Dark now, and Victoria has pulled into a gas station in Poughkeepsie, New York. Billy is under the hood with Gio as Victoria exits the convenience store with two bags of junk food. Gio looks around as discreetly as he can.

"He's across the street," Gio says.

"Go around the back of the store and get across the street. Don't get spotted."

"Done." Gio heads to the front of the convenience store but continues past it and disappears around the corner.

Randy is nervous and only watching Billy. He needs to call Freddy, but the only phone is by the nearby gas station. He sees Victoria eating in the front seat and Billy preoccupied under the hood. He may go unnoticed if he can quickly get to the pay phone by the storefront. Randy pops on a baseball cap for what little disguise he can muster and exits his truck quietly. As Randy crosses the street to the gas station, Gio crosses the street thirty feet down the road to get to Randy's truck. Billy can see Gio from the left corner of his eye. On his right periphery, he can see a man in a baseball cap heading to the pay phone. The lanky build gives Randy away, but Billy pretends not to notice him.

Randy has his back on Billy as he places a collect call to Freddy.

"Poughkeepsie. Him, his girlfriend, and Giovanni. I'll keep on him." Randy whispers into the phone.

While Randy is calling ahead, Gio makes quick work of Randy's back tires. Two deep punctures with a pocketknife and the rear of the truck drops. Gio goes across the street and heads back to Billy, who slams the hood shut. Gio hops in the back, and Billy takes over driving. The car starts and peels out of the station. Randy hangs up the telephone and darts across the street. He fires up his truck and immediately feels the inconsistency and unbalance. He stops and exits the truck to inspect. He sees the flats and throws his hat down.

"Goddammit!" Randy says through clenched teeth. He runs back across the street to the station and makes another phone call to Freddy.

Upstate New York is quite different from the bustling, loud and crowded southern section. Much of it is rolling hills lined with trees. The traffic is far less, and the long stretches of driving on the interstate can seem endless. Colgate Lake is twenty-odd miles west of the Catskills. The lake is fed by the East Kill River and is accessible from Route 78. The second Community is near the mouth of the river, where Billy, Victoria and Gio go on foot. A few miles in the dark on a narrow dirt path makes Victoria and Gio wonder if Billy is lost. Billy never wavers and keeps walking with purpose. Two hundred feet more, and there is a clearing, and they can see thirty trailers set in a large circle. Like Freddy's trailer at the Community in Toms River, Sam's trailer is situated dead center. The lights are off outside and in.

"They know we're coming. Gio, go around back and stay low."

Gio stays in the shadows created by the moonlight and moves to the back of Sam's trailer. Billy takes a step forward, but Victoria grabs his arm.

"What if it's a trap?"

"Then it's a trap. Stay here, and run back to the car if anything happens." Billy smiles at Victoria, and he goes to meet Gio. The two peek in the back window, but it's too dark to see anything. Gio takes one side of the metal mobile home, and Billy takes the other. The two meet in the front by the door. Billy walks up two steps to the front door, ready to kick it in, when he realizes that Sam's truck is missing. He knows they're gone. Billy turns the doorknob, and the door swings open. Once inside, Billy flicks on the light switch. It's filthy, with liquor bottles on every available surface. A cigar is still smoking in an ashtray. They were here an hour or so ago when Randy tipped them off. Gio and Billy check each room and find nothing of use.

"Now what? They can be anywhere." Gio says, looking around the cluttered living room.

The refrigerator's condenser kicks on, and Billy looks at the refrigerator door and sees photographs taped to the front of it. One photo catches his eye, and he moves closer to inspect it. The image is of Sam decked out in fishing gear holding a twenty-pound brown trout by a lake. Written in black marker is "CD LANE PARK 1994."

"Anything?" Gio asks.

"We're going fishing."

CD Lane Park sits ten miles north of the second Community. It is a scenic fishing and recreational park surrounded by the Catskill mountain range. It is closed to the public at night, but one of the park rangers is a friend of Sam's. For a certain amount of money and a certain amount of marijuana, Sam has unlimited access to the area. Billy, Victoria and Gio are at the edge of the 26-acre lake in the center of the park. There is a light wind, and the moonlight flickers off the ripples of the lake water. They scan across the lake and cannot see the other side. On the left, there are three small wooden buildings. The first is a store that rents sporting goods and fishing gear, and there are canoes for rent. The second is a lifeguard station for summer, and the third is a maintenance shed. The three walk towards the buildings. There is no sign of life anywhere, so it is easy for Billy and Gio to break into the first and third buildings and steal what they need. A baseball bat off the rack and a crossbow in a glass case were taken from the store. A machete and thirty feet of nylon cord from the maintenance shed. The three continue to circle the lake in search of Sam and Freddy. In the northern part of the lake, there is a dirt road leading up into the mountains. Billy kneels down with a lighter to examine tire tracks.

"They're here," Billy says.

"That could be anyone's truck. I think we should go. Sun will be up in a couple of hours." Gio says cautiously.

They find Sam's truck at four in the morning and two miles up the winding dirt track. The three quietly approach and look inside. It's empty. Off to the left, a faint yellow glow is deeper in the woods. A smaller, narrower track for foot traffic leads to a dying fire and two cheap polyester tents. One is blue, and the other is red. With the crossbow in tow, Gio circles around the back of the campsite while Billy and Victoria kneel in the brush. Two foxes scurry by them as if they suspect something bad. Billy grips the machete, Victoria holds the bat, and the rope is over her shoulder.

"You may see things you won't like. I'm sorry for bringing you." Billy whispers to Victoria.

"I knew what might happen. I'll follow you to the ends of the Earth, baby." Victoria looks into Billy's blue eyes with the firelight reflected in them. She almost forgets where they are until there is the sound of a tent being unzipped open. They turn to see Sam stumble out, clearly hungover. He is in boxer shorts and work boots, walks to a tree, and begins urinating. The crack of a branch causes Sam to stop midstream. He doesn't suspect a person but a bear. His hunting rifle is in his tent. Sam pulls up his boxer shorts and slowly walks towards his tent. The fear of being hunted sobers him quickly. Before he can bend down to get to his tent, there is a whooshing sound and pressure on the right side of his neck. An arrow has gone through it, and blood shoots from his mouth. He falls back into the nearly extinguished fire. Freddy immediately bursts from his tent and sees Sam struggling to pull the arrow from his neck. Freddy wrestles with Sam to get him off the fire and not pull the arrow out.

"Stop! You'll bleed out if you pull it. He's here." Freddy is measured and looking around in all directions while holding Sam's bloody hands as they grasp each end of the arrow. Gio emerges from the dark with the crossbow aimed at Freddy. Victoria is behind Gio with the bat and rope. Behind her is Billy dragging his machete on the ground to intimidate him. Freddy lets go of Sam's hands and stare at Billy. Sam pulls the arrow from his neck and begins to bleed furiously. The gagging and coughing crescendo as he chokes on his own blood.

"Put him out of his misery," Freddy tells Billy.

"Gio, listen to the man." Gio stands over Sam and shoots a second arrow into Sam's right eye. The spasms don't stop for a good minute.

People do not die like one sees in movies and television. There is a long, dragged-out procession of pain and struggle after an injury is inflicted. It's rare for someone to die instantly. Victoria can smell the burnt flesh on Sam's back as he lies dead near the fire. She feels nauseous and takes a few steps back from him.

"I'm not sure how you found me so quickly, William. You never fail to impress." Freddy is still on his knees while Gio has the crossbow on him, and William standing over him.

"What did you do to my mother?"

"What needed to be done. She became a liability. I know I can make you understand if I can explain it to you." Freddy is looking at Billy through his crooked, fogged-up glasses.

"You made your choice. The Community was more important than her. Now killing you is more important than keeping you alive." Billy says, pointing the tip of the machete between Freddy's eyes.

"You need to listen. You do not know the whole story. The future is yours, William, but you need to first get that blade out of my face." Freddy never blinks as he stares into Billy's eyes.

Billy lowers the machete. Gio has the crossbow focused on Freddy. Victoria shifts from Billy to Freddy, who begins to open his mouth to speak.

"Now, I…" A flash of pain hits Freddy in the mouth as he feels something heavy bounce off his chest. Victoria screams as she sees Freddy's mouth split open sideways from a strike of the machete. Freddy's tongue dangles grotesquely as his eyes roll back into his head. Most of Freddy's bottom jaw has been sliced off, which he felt roll down his chest. Freddy falls back, much like Sam and begins choking on his blood. Gio laughs a little as other sounds come from Freddy, who gropes at what is left of his face. The other sounds that Freddy emotes are words that are, of course, unintelligible. Billy just watches.

"Put him down," Billy says.

Gio stands over Freddy and shoots an arrow into Freddy's forehead. After an eternity of silence, the crickets begin registering in Victoria's ears. She turns her back to the carnage, and her eyes begin to well up. She holds the nylon rope tight.

"You were supposed to tie him up and question him. That was the plan. Why did you do that?" She asks.

Billy walks to Victoria and talks to the back of her head. She wipes away tears.

"He's a liar. He was going to tell me nothing. I came here to do what I had to. He went quickly. I owed him that much. We need to go." Billy looks to Gio, who is taking Sam's rifle and truck keys from the tent.

"People will notice we have been gone. We have to use Sam's truck. We'll swap it out again the further west we go." Billy tells them.

"Where are we going?" Gio asks.

"California," Billy says, still looking at the back of Victoria's head. She cannot look at either of them.

"California?" Gio asks, confused.

"We need more people," Billy says, looking up at the crescent Moon.

"For what?"

Billy turns to Gio and smirks.

"We're starting over. It will be different, bigger, and better. Freddy's dream was small and corrupted by greed. This time we are going to do it right." Billy starts to walk the trail leading back to Sam's truck. Gio follows behind, and eventually, so does Victoria.

Chapter 19

May, 1998

Laura is sitting at the kitchen table doing a crossword puzzle. She hears the apartment's front door unlock, and Michael enters after work.

"What's for dinner?" He asks.

"You're a grown man now. Get your own. You work, and you have money. I want you to start doing your own laundry too. I'm not a maid." Laura never looks at her son, only at her puzzle. She's trying to figure out a seven-letter word for ABANDON. Michael says nothing and walks to his room. He lays down on the bed, puts on some headphones, and listens to "Green Man" by Type O Negative. The song is about a fictional character born in Spring and dies in Winter. He fumbles under his bed and takes out his stolen Bible. The anger towards his mother subsides as he reads Matthew 4: 1-11, which details Satan's attempt to corrupt Jesus in the desert.

Laura finally figures out the seven-letter word for ABANDON is NEGLECT. She fails to see the irony.

The following morning Paul is at the beginning of his driveway with a push broom and three buckets of seal coat. The driveway is twenty-five feet long and leads to his detached garage. Michael had power washed the driveway the day before. A large crack that runs the whole length of the driveway has split almost six inches in a jagged line. Paul had thought of hiring someone to repair it, but the desire to save a few dollars won out. The humidity is already making Paul sweat. Paul doubts he can seal the entire length in one coat. He will start by the garage with the brush and work his way down to the end. There is no shade, so Paul wants to work quickly to avoid the noonday sun.

An hour has passed, and two-thirds of the driveway has one coat. Paul is drenched in sweat. The veins in his temples are throbbing, and he begins to see stars. He blinks and shakes his head to clear them. He knows he needs a break, so he walks to the property's fence line and leans against the wooden boards. He is still holding the broom, which has a wooden handle. He wonders how many trees it took to build this fence, the frame of his house and the handle of the broom he holds. He wonders if the wood came from the same forest. Paul looks up at the sun and the cloudless blue sky. The blue makes him think of the ocean. He can hear waves crashing, which is replaced by a loud whooshing sound. His head feels light, and there is a terrible heavy pain in his chest. He clutches at his heart and vomits on his freshly sealed driveway. Paul falls into his own vomit and loses consciousness.

The emergency room at Toms River Community Hospital has a waiting area. It's quiet and almost cozy. The floors are carpeted, and the chairs are cushioned. Four televisions are set in the room's upper corners with daytime television programming on. A young Mexican mother sits in the waiting area with a toddler on her lap. She plays with her mother's golden crucifix around her neck. In the center sits a middle-aged woman next to her elderly mother in a wheelchair and an oxygen mask. On the opposite side of the room are Laura and Michael.

"You should have coated the driveway yourself." Laura is agitated and adjusts her glasses.

Laughter comes from a room behind the reception area. It is far too loud and feels inappropriate for this setting. It rubs the few people in the waiting area the wrong way. A small, chubby woman with red hair exits from the back wearing a doctor's coat. Her smile quickly turns to a concerned look as she approaches Laura and Michael. Her concerned look seems rehearsed to Laura.

"Mrs. Phy?" She asks.

"Krueger. We never married. Is he going to be alright?"

"He's sedated. It was a major cardiac episode. Ninety percent blockages in all four arteries. We were able to open them back up with angioplasty. You can see him if you like, but he is not conscious. Visiting hours end at seven tonight."

"Thank you, doctor." Laura gets up to follow the doctor, and Michael follows behind. Through two swinging doors and past a security guard, the halls of the ICU are brightly lit, white, and sterile. A young nurse in blue scrubs is walking in the opposite direction. She smiles at the doctor and Laura but looks away when she sees Michael and his left eye. When someone cannot make direct eye contact with a person, it can be jarring and unsettling. Michael is used to these types of reactions.

The last room down the hall is Paul's. He is alone and hooked up to a respirator. Laura sits next to him, and Michael sits by the window. Laura cannot bring herself to cry, but she is concerned. It surprises her how much she is concerned. Michael looks out the window and watches cars pull in and out of the parking garage across the way. There are no words spoken or sounds in the room except for the beeping of a heart monitor.

At around this time and three miles south in downtown, Clarence Gardener is sitting on the front porch of his one-story house. James is sitting next to him and watching his nephew. Thomas is playing in the front yard jumping through a lawn sprinkler in cut-off jean shorts.

"Do you remember Fred Bile from Pine Acres?" James asks his father.

"Of course."

"Was found dead near the Catskills. Murdered."

"Any suspects? I'm sure he's made plenty of enemies over the years."

"William Mallek and possibly two others. They went missing after Mallek's mother disappeared. I guess he blamed Bile for that."

"Don't get caught up in it. I know you get hyper-focused on things. It's out of your jurisdiction."

"I know. I won't." James watches Thomas jump through the sprinkler. His eyes drift up to a black cloud off to the west. His mood becomes sullen as the feelings in his stomach churn.

"Are you worried about something?" Clarence asks his son.

"I just don't see things getting better around here."

"More people bring more problems. It's a growing town. You can't control it all. You do the job to the best of your abilities, and you make sure you get home every night. That's the most important part. I felt the same way you do now."

"How did you deal with it?"

"I didn't. I just counted the days until retirement." Clarence takes a sip of iced tea. He places the glass down as he watches Thomas. "The Devil preys on the young and the weak. Protect them first."

"How do I find out where the Devil is hiding?"

"Follow your instincts and watch the animals."

"Watch the animals?" James asks.

"Some say animals have a sixth sense. They know and can see things we can't. Just watch them. Their behavior can predict dark days ahead." Clarence takes another sip.

James takes his father's words to heart even if he doesn't quite understand them. James looks up and can see more dark clouds on the western horizon.

Monday afternoon, and still no change in Paul's condition. Laura is sitting at his bedside doing a crossword puzzle. Laura remembers giving birth eighteen years ago in this hospital. Memory pains in her abdomen hit. The cause of that pain is Michael, who walks into the room. He has just come from a power washing job, and his clothes are still damp. He sits by the window and looks at some blisters forming on his palms around his thumbs and forefinger. He knows he should wear gloves to work but wants the blisters to turn into calluses for tougher hands. Michael goes to his rear pocket and takes out a piece of scrap paper. On the paper is Saint Michael's Prayer. He picked it for the name. A Prayer for the Sick would have been more appropriate, but Michael hasn't discovered it.

"What's that?" Laura asks.

"A prayer."

"Prayer? You don't believe in all that nonsense, do you? They're fairy tales."

"Couldn't hurt," Michael says, never looking at his mother.

"Don't let it warp your mind."

Paul's consciousness was black, but the sounds of the words from Laura and Michael broke through. He slips back into nothing, but there are now flashes as the neurons in his brain begin to fire. The flashes contain images. One image is of his father's face. The next is the squirrel he killed as a boy. Another is a radiant image of a teenage Laura. A flash of his son as a baby with his deformed eye. The last image is of Michael with an emaciated, almost skeletal face, with black blood coming from his mouth.

Paul begins to make a gurgling noise. Laura and Michael get up and go to him. His eyes begin to open.

"Paul, it's Laura and Michael. You're okay. You're at the hospital." Laura says with genuine concern that Paul hadn't heard in years.

Toward the end of his shift, James decides to take a detour before punching out at the precinct. He pulls up to the house in Lakehurst that Victoria Black lived in with her mother. The house is in the poor part of town. Yellow police tape is across the front door. Since the discovery of Frederick Bile and Sam Betancourt's bodies, all of the suspects' homes have been searched. They will continue to be searched for evidence of the whereabouts of the persons in question. Giovanni Gomez's parents' home is currently going through a search and seizure by authorities. Victoria Black's mother lives in a hotel two miles down the road. James enters the home to satisfy a curiosity. His steps are deliberate and cautious. He is not a detective, so he should not be here. James goes from room to room just to get a feel for how Victoria lives. It isn't until he gets to her bedroom that he can get a real sense of who she is. Black curtains, black sheets, black candles, heavy metal and horror movie posters on the walls, and music discs scattered on the floor. One poster gets his attention. It is hung on the ceiling directly over the bed. It's a movie poster for the film "The Lost Boys." James has seen the movie and knows it centers around teenage vampires living in California. If James were a betting man, which he is not, he would guess that the three suspects, Victoria Black, Giovanni Gomez and William Mallek, are headed west. James exits the bedroom and thinks of something his father told him the day before his first day at the academy.

"When people are lost, they follow anyone that gives them a purpose. Sometimes they follow the wrong people who make them do bad things. With this job, you will see the bad, which can be scary. The trick is not to be scared because you know some good is left. You be good." Clarence's words have stuck with James ever since. They help when he feels overwhelmed and hopeless. As James pulls away from Victoria Black's home, he feels more overwhelmed and hopeless than ever.

Four days have passed, and Paul is ready to go home. The doctors are encouraged by his recent tests and feel confident to discharge him from the hospital with one caveat. He needs a caretaker for two weeks. Laura volunteered. She is pushing Paul's wheelchair to her car, parked with hazard lights blinking out in front of the exit doors.

"How are you feeling?" Laura asks.

"Weak."

Laura helps Paul, who is still a big man despite losing weight in the hospital, into the passenger seat, and she goes around to the driver's side. She helps him with his seatbelt and pulls away.

"Where's Michael?" Paul asks.

"At work. I told him to take off, but he didn't listen."

Driving to Paul's house, there is little conversation. When they get to Paul's house, he sees that someone finished coating the driveway while he was gone.

"Looks good."

"Michael finished it for you," Laura says, stopping her car in front of the house. "Still too wet to drive on, though."

Laura gets out and goes to the passenger side to help Paul out of the car. Inside the house, it is quiet and musty. Laura helps Paul to the couch and opens some windows to let air in. Paul is happy about the attention he is getting, and Laura feels a sense of purpose and usefulness. They are feelings that neither of them has had in years. Sometimes a tragedy brings people closer and makes them realize what is important, or it could just be a fleeting moment of familiarity. Either way, it was a different and good day, and they will take that. Paul sits comfortably on the sofa and takes the Asbury Park Press off the coffee table. The local news section of the paper has an article about a local landowner who was found murdered in New York. The landowner was Frederick Bile. It has been years since Paul has seen Freddy. Paul is indifferent to the news.

Michael has his work truck parked on a desolate dirt road in the southern town of Lacey Township. Lacey is not as developed as Toms River, and there are many acres of wooded lands, dirt roads, and hidden trails. There is even a Crystal Lake hidden off Bone Hill Road with completely clear water supplied by a freshwater spring. It attracts a lot of attention from locals who know about it and is now off limits and cut off by NO TRESPASSING signs. Michael is not parked far from there. He sits quietly in his truck with the windows down and reads his scarred Bible. One passage is resonating with him at the moment. It is from Deuteronomy 32:35 "Vengeance is Mine, and retribution, in due time their foot will slip; for the day of their calamity is near, and the impending things are hastening upon them." Michael highlights this with a yellow marker. He fails to distinguish that "Mine" refers to Christ, not himself. It is an unfortunate error. Michael hears some rustling in the trees and closes his Bible to look. He sees two squirrels running and chasing each other. He can't tell if it is for play or for mating. He wonders what squirrel tastes like and how he would kill one. A gun is too easy. Perhaps a slingshot like his father used to have as a boy.

The next afternoon Laura is shopping at the grocery store she works. She is looking for steaks to cook tonight for Paul. It reminds her of the years she would cook for the family. She never liked cooking, but the routine is what she finds comforting. She knows Paul prefers a thicker steak and is picking out the best one. The years of being a single mother have not been kind to Laura. Men don't look her way anymore. She is only in her mid-thirties but looks much older. Smoking, working, and stress have taken their toll quickly. She misses the attention Paul gave her as a teenager. She misses the attention male customers at the grocery would give her in her twenties. Laura knows that these are her invisible years. She looks and feels like a middle-aged woman and feels that she is no longer desirable. It hurts, but now she has a man to take care of. Even if it is a man, she left and doesn't love. She picks the thickest and bloodiest steak and puts it in her shopping cart.

Chapter 20

May, 1998

Dayton, Ohio, is where Sam Betancourt's truck is now. It is parked in the lot of a cheap

motel off Route 4. The truck will not leave here. It will be searched by police in two days when

the manager at the motel calls it in. Its former occupants will be in another stolen vehicle headed

west by then. For now, however, it sits quietly at night, parked in front of room 6. That is where

Billy, Victoria, and Gio stay. Sitting on the bed is Victoria. Her eyes widen as she watches Gio

count thousands of dollars in cash from a camouflage duffle bag. The bag was under the rear

passenger seat of Sam's pickup. The second Community had generated money through petty

crime in upstate New York. It was now in the hands of three fugitives.

"At least twenty grand. More than enough to get us to California." Gio says.

Victoria is half excited at the prospect of being in California with tens of thousands of

dollars and half worried that the police could bust down the door at any moment. She is now

distracted by the fact that Billy has been in the bathroom for over thirty minutes. She hears a

rough, grating sound coming from the bathroom. She knocks on the door.

"You okay, baby?" She asks while hearing Billy spit.

"Never better. Come in." Billy says.

Victoria opens the door and sees Billy with his shirt off in front of the bathroom mirror.

She glances down and can see white foam and blood in the sink. She then looks up at Billy's face

in the bathroom mirror. She sees a ghastly sight. Billy has used a metal file from the stolen truck to file down his teeth, except for the cuspids. He has given himself fangs. Victoria has no words, and Gio pokes his head in to see.

"Dude, what the fuck?"

"You're next. Then Vic." Billy says, pointing at the metal file on the bathroom counter.

"I don't even like the dentist. I'm not doing that." Gio tells Billy while backing away from the bathroom.

"You want to belong, then you have to look the part. It's only bone, Gio."

Victoria reaches for the file and runs her fingers over the rough grooves of it. She is intrigued and also hesitant. It would show Billy that she is committed to him. However, it will be a painful and irreversible gesture. She feels guilt after questioning his handling of Freddy. After a couple of days, the shock of the murder wore off. She never apologized for questioning Billy's choice, so she thinks joining him in this would be enough of an apology.

"I'll do it." Victoria grabs the file. Gio looks down at the floor in shame. Billy stands behind Victoria as she puts the file to her mouth. Gio walks to the bed of the motel. He sits down and puts his head in his hands. He knows he will do what Billy wants.

A 1985 Black Buick Regal T-Type is sitting on the side of Grove Avenue in Dayton. It is a quiet residential street. A red and white FOR SALE BY OWNER sign is on the windshield. It's night, and the street lamp above protects it from would-be thieves. These are not ordinary thieves. An arrow from a crossbow shoots out the street light. The front door is unlocked in two minutes, and the engine turns over. Years of stealing cars for the Community in Toms River have made Billy and Gio quite adept at these nocturnal activities. Victoria is switching the license plates out with plates stolen from an abandoned tractor in Pennsylvania. It won't be for another ten hours that the owner will report the car stolen, and our three thieves will have different plates in different states.

The next few days on the road seem like a blur of farmland, small towns, gas stations and cheap motels. The trio sticks to back roads and avoids driving at peak hours of the day. They have become accustomed to sleeping all day and driving all night. They are nearing the Kansas border when Gio offers an idea.

"Why not just say fuck it and go to Mexico? We can live like kings there."

"Mexico could be cool," Victoria adds.

Billy says nothing. He grips the steering wheel tighter and concentrates on the road. It is night, and he is wearing sunglasses. They come to a stop light, and a minivan with a child in the front passenger seat looks over at the blacked-out Buick with tinted windows.

"Death Valley is where we go. If it fails, then I'll think about Mexico." Billy lowers his car window and looks at the child in the car next to him. The child stares back at him with an innocent round face and blue eyes. Billy pulls down his sunglasses to show him his blue eyes. Billy then smiles at the boy showing him his frightening grimace. The boy's eyes widen, and he quickly looks forward, avoiding the sight. Billy's sunglasses go back on, and the car window rolls up. "Supernova" by Liz Phair comes on the rock station. The light turns green, and the Buick takes off, but not above the speed limit. Billy wants to stay invisible to authorities. To Gio and Victoria, the idea of Death Valley is risky. They are wanted for murder, and to stay in the states is dangerous. Setting up another Community in an unfamiliar part of the country will be daunting, but to Billy, it will be paradise. What Billy wants, he gets.

Saturday afternoon at CD Lane Park is empty. The park is open, but the recent murders here have scared the locals off. James is off today and made the three-plus hour drive to New York. He is alone and here for one reason, to satisfy his curiosity. James has always been inquisitive by nature. As a boy, he would study his fellow students and adjust his behavior accordingly to avoid conflicts. James was small growing up and did what he could to avoid confrontations with other boys in class. At home, he would ask his father questions about his day. He was fascinated by police work and by his father out there catching the bad guys. So, when James learned of the murder site of Frederick Bile and Samuel Betancourt, he hopped in his car early in the morning and drove up. He had questions that needed answers. He gets to the lake and sees three buildings. The sports equipment store has plywood over the windows from the recent break-in. The maintenance shed has two heavy chains across the door secured with a padlock. James continues to walk around the edge of the lake and thinks this would be a nice place to fish with his nephew. James is really interested in the opening in the woods at the far end, with orange cones and yellow police tape marking it off. The murder site is through there. The park is empty, and James did bring his badge in case local police or a park ranger asked him about his business. No one bothers him. The woods are dark and musty. There was a wind by the lake, but there was not even a breeze here. James gets to the campsite, and it is also marked off with tape. The tents are gone and in evidence. The decayed campfire was the only thing to signify any human presence had been here. James is curious how driven William Mallek must have been to travel all this way. To find such a remote campsite and then kill two men. He had help. The question of why they helped William commit these crimes is intriguing. *What kind of hold does he have over them? What bonds them together? Is it a cult? Do they really believe they are vampires?* The questions gnaw at him. He imagines the murders. Just yesterday, in the Toms River Precinct's Homicide Division, he could glance at the autopsy photos posted on a bulletin board in one of the detective's offices. He saw the pictures of the large wound to the neck of Betancourt and the lower jaw missing from Bile.

James leaves the crime scene and can feel the wickedness and evil that happened there. It is in the quiet. It is in the trees. A numb sort of heaviness that makes footsteps heavier and breathing labored. James is out of the woods and by the lake. He just wants to get to his car and go back home. Not that home is much better. There is something malicious there as well. The Devil and his legions are all around, always watching and waiting. To avoid them, you must be mindful and pay them no mind. It is a high-wire act that the faithful must balance, and one false step or bad choice can lead to dark fallen days.

James is on the parkway south and headed home. Tomorrow is Sunday, and he will be going to church with his nephew. He will take Thomas fishing afterward. Island Beach State Park is their favorite spot for striped bass. One thing is for certain after today, James will never take his nephew fishing in upstate New York.

Sunday, during mass, James feels inadequate. Church can make a person feel that way sometimes. *Am I worthy enough? Should I volunteer more? Is there a sin I haven't repented for?* It is a feeling that haunts James at work and in the quiet moments of life. He wonders if he is good at his job. He has doubts if he has what it takes to graduate to detective and achieve his goal of joining the Federal Bureau of Investigation. In his empty apartment at night, he questions if his decisions to be single and childless were correct. The feeling of inadequacy is something that he needs to purge. It does no good, much like the seven deadly sins. These feelings of inadequacy offer nothing and can cripple a person emotionally, spiritually and even physically. James tries to concentrate on the mass. The sermon is given by Father Reddy, a man of Indian descent who converted to Catholicism when he emigrated to America thirty years ago. The sermon centers around what we are working towards and what more we can do.

"To love as Christ loved is a good start." Father Reddy finishes his sermon. Then there is

Communion, and to conclude the service is St. Michael's Prayer.

"Saint Michael, the Archangel, defends us in battle. Be our protection against the wickedness and snares of the Devil. May God rebuke him, we humbly pray; and do thou, O Prince of the Heavenly Host, by the power of God, thrust into Hell Satan and all the evil spirits who wander through the world for the ruin of souls. Amen." The congregation recites.

James is driving Thomas home. People assume that Thomas is his son. Sometimes James does feel like his father. He wanted at least one child but was never very good at selecting possible mates. His first girlfriend in high school cheated on him with the varsity quarterback. In his twenties, another girlfriend lost herself to pills and alcohol. Since then, he has dated sparingly, but women are selective in choosing men. Women want providers and someone who has more earning potential than themselves. A cop is a noble profession, but it doesn't pay well. James is also sullen. Women can tell there is something behind his brown eyes. A sort of fog or depression. Either they lose interest in him, or he loses interest in them. He is alone by choice and by circumstance.

"Are there really demons, Uncle James?" Thomas asks.

"Yes," James answers without hesitation.

"Should I be scared?"

"Yes, but you have family and faith on your side, so don't be too scared. It's something we all have to deal with." James says, trying to comfort his nephew.

"What do demons look like? How can we see them?"

"They can look like you and me. Just regular people. That's why we have to be careful about who we meet and let into our lives. Don't live in fear, Tommy. Just be aware."

"Can we go fishing now?" Thomas asks.

"Yes, we can go fishing now."

Monday morning is brisk and breezy, especially on the boardwalk of Seaside Heights. It is Memorial Day, and Michael chose to work instead of celebrating the holiday. Packed with locals and tourists from New York and Pennsylvania, it was difficult for Michael to park his work truck. He parked at the free parking lot one mile from the boardwalk. He lugs the power washer behind him and is thankful it has wheels. A pizzeria at the far north end of the boardwalk had an overflowing toilet which destroyed the bathroom's floor and walls. The owners called and offered double the price because of the holiday. The crowds of people on the streets and the boardwalk make Michael uneasy, especially when some people stare at him, lugging the heavy power washer with squeaky wheels. Michael gets to the pizzeria and notices the pretty young brunette at the counter. Michael makes eye contact with her, and she quickly looks away. She points to the bathroom in the back of the parlor. Michael is used to the awkwardness between him and the girls. It still hurts his feelings when they look at him oddly or not at all.

The bathroom is covered in filth. A big industrial fan is blowing the odor out of the open back door. Most would be disgusted and refuse this job, but Michael just goes to work with little hesitation. The best way to finish a terrible job like this is to have your mind preoccupied. Michael thinks of the stories he's read in the Bible. The misinterpreted ones. As the filth is being sprayed off the linoleum tiles and down the center drain trap in the floor, he cannot help but make the correlation to filth being wiped clean from his life. Michael always felt that his mind was corrupted and dirty. Ugly voices and thoughts would come and go. They could be unsettling and so frightening that he has spent most of his waking life trying to silence them. He banishes them to a place he calls the "void." It is similar to a black hole. It is located in the far reaches of his conscious self and swallows everything whole, including morality, reasoning and intelligence. The lexicon to describe his thoughts in the "void" does not exist, so we'll go no further.

As Michael pulls the power washer back to his work truck, he feels more confident. He is stronger, more independent, earning money and occasionally receives praise for his work. His father thanked him for the good job he did finishing the driveway. Michael doesn't remember when his father said he did something good. He had never heard it from his mother.

Laura is taking Paul's clothes out of the dryer at his home.

"This is only for two weeks. I hope you know!" She shouts to Paul in the next room.

"I know."

Laura doesn't really mind doing Paul's laundry while he recovers. She puts up a strong front to him out of defense. To convince him she is not coming back and to also convince herself. It was nice to be needed again. Not that Laura enjoyed doing chores. She just enjoyed the feeling of people depending on her for something. Michael hadn't depended on her recently. She felt him becoming distant. More time at work, more time away from home. When he is home, he hides in his room, listening to music and reading his Bible. She never really knew her son, and now she knew him even less, and that thought is what scared her. She is reminded of a dream she had recently. She was out swimming by herself at the beach. It was early dawn, and the ocean felt cold. She felt helpless. She couldn't feel the sand under her feet and was out too far. She tried swimming back to shore but was dragged further and further out. She was tired and looked down at her hands. They were pruned and wrinkled, but not from the saltwater. She was old and alone and helpless, drifting at sea.

As Laura folded clothes in the living room, she watched Paul lying on the couch watching television. He was half asleep. She toyed with the idea of sleeping over. Laura didn't want to go back to the apartment she shared with her son. It didn't feel safe anymore. Passing grunts in the

hallway and no talk during dinner began to erode her sense of home. She slept with her bedroom

door locked. It was as if she were a child again, unable to sleep without a night light or having
the

closet door open. She would always get up and close it, even now as an adult. The cavernous

black opening staring at her night made her think of monsters. The last thing she needed was a

monster in her closet when she might have a monster.

Chapter 21

June, 1998

Traveling west on Interstate 70 in Colorado is the Black Buick Regal. The plates have been swapped out so often that Billy has lost count. Bouncing from small town to small town on back roads for multiple weeks has been tough. The three travelers are road weary, but the goal is less than a thousand miles away. A day and a half more of travel and they should be there. Gio is in the backseat trying to sleep. He can't. The fear of getting caught is getting the better of him. It is also getting the better of Billy. He knows it's only a matter of time until they get caught. Billy is desperately chasing a dream of starting his own Community in California. Nothing can get in the way of that. Especially the Colorado State Trooper that is behind them. Billy maintains the speed limit. The tinted windows are not helping, but he can do nothing about that.

Victoria stares out the passenger side window at the snow-capped Rocky Mountains. It is breathtaking, but the miles and the days on the road are taking their toll on her. She cannot believe that she is actually feeling homesick. *Homesick for Jersey? Look at this view. You're never getting back home. Maybe it's best that I don't.* She is so lost in her mind that she doesn't notice the state trooper in her passenger side mirror. Gio sits up in the back and rubs his jaw. The teeth filing didn't go well, and he may have removed too much enamel. His bite is also off, causing the pain. He notices Billy looking in the rearview mirror.

"Don't turn around," Billy says to Gio.

"Let me guess. A cop is behind us." Gio says, and Victoria straightens up in her seat.

"He's been on us for the last three miles."

"Billy, I told you we should fucking bolt to Mexico."

"Maybe Gio's right. What will we say to a cop when he pulls us over, and we look like this?" For the first time, Victoria is scared, and Billy doubts her commitment to him.

"The plan doesn't change. No cop is getting in the way of that." As Billy says this, the trooper gets into the left passing lane and pops on his lights. Everyone's heart sinks until the trooper blows past them. He is responding to another call.

"Christ. What is this master plan in California that we are risking everything for" Gio asks?

"There's a new revolution coming. We go and recruit and build a place of our very own that is incorruptible. A place where we can operate without interference and grow so big that people from all over the country will come. We're going to Death Valley." Billy says. No one else in the car says a word. Billy can sense their confidence in him is waning. He knows he must prove to them how real this can be. He needs to show Gio and, more importantly, Victoria how far he is willing to go. Billy is ready to take that next step into ascension, and when they see, they will believe and follow him to the end.

Victoria always wanted to visit Las Vegas. She didn't imagine it would be under these circumstances. There isn't a direct way to get to Death Valley without first taking Interstate 15 and then connecting to Route 95 in the middle of Las Vegas. The Buick sticks out like a sore thumb as it cruises through the strip past new-model luxury cars, limousines and sports cars. This is the last place Billy wants to be.

"Take a good look while you can because we need to get out of here fast," Billy tells his partners.

"I guess we're not going to take in a show," Gio says, trying to lighten the mood.

Victoria looks at all the people going up and down the Vegas strip at dusk - tourists, locals, families and police. She flirts with the idea of jumping out of the car and just running away, but she can't. Despite everything, the murders, the guilt, the insanity of it all, she can't leave Billy. Her heart and body ache for him. She will stay with him - for now.

Gio would rather stop at a motel and see a little of Las Vegas, but he knows that is an impossibility. The sooner they are away from flashing neon lights, the better. If worse came to worse, Gio would stay with Billy with guns drawn and go out like "Butch Cassidy and the Sundance Kid." Gio feels that he and Billy are brothers from another life. He had this revelation two years ago while dropping acid behind a liquor store in Jersey.

The next night, with Nevada now behind them, they cross over the state line into California. The sky is pink and purple behind them and pitch black in front. Mountain ranges and signs warning of EXTREME HEAT are spotted, as is a sign that reads DEATH VALLEY STRAIGHT AHEAD. The three have arrived at their destination. Tomorrow they will look for shelter here and stock up on food and water. They have plenty of Sam and Freddy's money to get them started. After they get settled in, Billy will begin to enact the plans he has been drawing up in his mind. He has a headache and needs sleep. He will drive in and stop the car on the first dirt road on the right. Death Valley is a national park but so large that many can go unnoticed for days and weeks. Billy knows he can't live inside the park, but you can on the outskirts. The dry weather and heat keep the population low, and with fewer people come fewer curious eyes. A perfect spot for a new Community. Billy's Community.

Up ahead on the right is a road. Billy takes it. A little further down another road, he takes that. He parks behind some dead brush. Victoria and Gio are already asleep, and Billy closes his eyes to join them.

The next morning the three head to the small town of Tecopa near Death Valley. Billy and Gio gas up the Buick while Victoria goes into town to buy bottled water and food. They figure a woman would not intimidate any local shop owners. Get in and get out is the plan this morning. When afternoon comes, they park the Buick in the shade of the Greenwater Mountain Range. They get out and walk the trails and valleys. The heat is oppressive and well over one hundred degrees. Gio is sure he will suffer from heatstroke if they don't stop soon. Gio is carrying a black army sack over his shoulder, which holds the rifle they got from Sam, the crossbow, machete, and rope.

"This is dangerous. We're going to die out here." Victoria says, taking a swig from her bottled water.

"We should go out at night," Gio adds.

"We will, but we don't stop until we find it." Billy takes a run up ahead and stands on a boulder. He looks down into a valley and scans it carefully. Barren, with many small cactus and random wildflower patches. Nestled across the valley at the feet of the Greenwater Mountains are a two-story, white wooden farmhouse and a barn. Tiny but isolated. One black wire is connected to a utility pole up the side. Billy fixates on the house, looking for any signs of life, including cars around the area. He sees nothing.

"Down there," Billy says. Victoria and Gio stand next to him and look at where he is pointing.

"What if someone is in there?" Victoria asks.

"We just say we're lost, hikers." Billy starts heading down. Gio follows quickly behind. Victoria waits and relents. She follows them down the range into the valley below.

The walk is at least two miles, and the heat makes it feel like ten. Under the creosote bushes that litter the valley could be spiders, scorpions and any number of species of snake. The three walk cautiously. Covered in sweat, they make it to the farmhouse's front porch. Too hot and weary for any clever entry, Billy simply knocks on the door. Gio peeks in the front window and sees nothing inside, not even furniture. Victoria looks to the right and behind the farmhouse and sees the barn. The front doors of the old wooden structure swing open in the breeze.

"No one here." Billy turns the doorknob and pushes open the door. He breaks the old metal lock from the hinges. He stands in the doorway, waiting for a noise or someone running down the stairs. There is nothing. The three enter and walk through the house slowly. Just a break from the sun makes it feel twenty degrees cooler inside. Billy goes into each room on the first floor while Victoria goes to the kitchen. Gio is exhausted and sits in the corner of the first room. He pours the little water left from his bottle onto his head. In a moment of clarity, Gio thinks, *Who locked the front door?*

Inside the kitchen, the wallpaper is faded and green. There are faint pictures of flower baskets on them. The wooden countertops are varnished and heavy looking. There is a steady drip of water coming from the kitchen sink. She exits the kitchen and sees a pink rotary phone in the hallway on a cheap hardwood table. Victoria can't help but pick up the receiver on the phone. She hears a dial tone and hangs up. She moves down the hallway to see where Billy went, and then she stops and has a realization—dial *tone. The water is on. Someone is staying here. Why no furniture?* Before she can reach Billy, she sees him hurrying down the stairs.

"There's a truck coming," Billy says as he makes for the door. Victoria hurries behind him, and Gio gets up with the sack over his shoulder, but it's too late. The pickup truck stops in front of the farmhouse. Billy, Victoria and Gio are on the front porch and stare through the truck's front windshield and see a man, a woman and a girl sitting in the front seat. The man pauses and puts the truck in park. He exits the truck, and the squeakiness of the rusted-out truck door gives Victoria an uneasy feeling in her stomach.

"Why are you in my house?" The man asks.

The man is Martin Chuska. His wife is Maria, and his daughter is Summer. The family owns a horse farm three miles away in Tecopa. He and his wife recently purchased this property in hopes of expansion. They offer tours of the national park on horseback. Martin and Maria are both of partial Native American descent. Martin and Maria are one-quarter Mojave. Martin bought the home, paid for the utilities to be turned on and was planning on furnishing the house in a few days. Today they wanted to clean out the barn for their three Appaloosa horses, but the three strangers on their front porch have changed their plans.

"Sorry, we were out hiking and got lost. This is the first place we've seen in two days." Billy says.

"Hiking? Dressed like that?" Martin looks at their boots and tattered jeans. He also notices their strange teeth. The cuspids are more pronounced.

"We lost our campsite." Billy knows this man doesn't believe him.

"You broke my front door." Martin looks at his wife and, with his eyes, clues her to the glove compartment in the truck. Maria opens the compartment and takes out a bulldog revolver. Her hands shake as she feels for her grip. She keeps it low, so the three intruders can't see. Summer is scared and keeps her eyes on the black bag over the second man's shoulder.

"I suggest you three leave the way you came. If I see you again, I'm calling the police. Got it?" Martin is stern outwardly, but inside, his stomach is sinking. The man with the bag keeps looking at his wife in the truck. *He knows she has a gun. I pray he doesn't have one. Let my family make it through this.*

"Well, there is a problem," Billy says. He glances to Gio on his left and Victoria to his right. "You've seen our faces."

"What's that supposed to mean?" Martin asks, knowing full well what that means.

Gio lets the sack slip off his shoulder to the porch. It makes a heavy clunking sound.

"It means we should probably all go inside and talk about this." Billy tilts his head to the left, and in one simple motion, Gio drops to one knee and pulls out the rifle from the sack. He points it directly at Maria in the front seat. Her heart jumps, and she pulls up the revolver to shoot through the windshield. There is a shot, but it is not from the revolver. Gio has blasted out the windshield as Summer screams. Martin dives into the front seat and tries to grab the revolver from Maria's hand.

"Don't move! Next time my friend won't miss!" Billy shouts. Gio has the rifle pointed at the front seat of the truck. The Chuskas have their heads down. Victoria ran inside the house after the shot.

"Make them show their hands," Gio says.

"Let's see your hands! All six of them, and there better not be a gun in one of them!" Billy keeps his eyes locked on the truck's dashboard, hoping to see six empty hands raise up over it. One by one, all six hands come up over the dashboard. While he watches, he goes to the black sack and takes out his machete and rope.

"Now get out of the truck slowly, and let's go inside! If you try anything brave, my friend will not hesitate to make this a very bad day!"

Martin is the first to exit the truck with his hands in the air. Next is Summer, with tears coming down her cheeks and bits of glass in her dirty blonde hair. Last, from the passenger side, comes Maria with her eyes fixed on the fallen revolver on the front seat. Being lost at sea and unable to get to the life raft only feet away. The feeling is similar. Maria goes around the front of the truck and stands with her family. Her stare is now focused on the long barrel of Gio's rifle.

"Inside. Slowly." Billy keeps a keen eye on Martin. A father's instinct is to protect his family at all costs. Billy would do the same. The Chuskas walk inside with Billy and Gio behind them. Under Billy's direction and Gio's rifle, they all sit in a semicircle. Billy cuts up the nylon rope with his machete and makes Maria tie Martin and Summer's hands. He examines to make sure the knots are tight. Victoria has crept into the room to watch.

"Tie her now," Billy tells Victoria. His voice echoes off the walls of the empty house.

Victoria has also been crying but does what Billy says. She ties Maria's wrists together and curiously goes into the kitchen.

"You don't have a plan, do you, young man?" Martin asks.

"Well, we can sit here all night until I figure one out."

"You can leave. This doesn't have to go any further. You and your friends can take my truck, and you would have a day head start. You can get anywhere in a day. You still have choices. My only option is to beg and plead with you to leave us be." Martin is making direct eye contact with Billy, who is standing over him.

"I'd like to, but you and I both know I can't do that."

"Do you have a mother? A father?" Martin asks.

"She's gone. These two with me are my family now, and this was going to be our home. Now it can't. If only you had arrived a little sooner, we would have passed this place by and found something else, but now here we are." Billy holds opposing thoughts in him. He doesn't want to kill an entire family, but this family will put him behind bars for the rest of his life. He believes to be biding his time, but in reality, he is just procrastinating the inevitable. He must kill the father first. Billy just doesn't have the nerve yet, and for his own reasons, he will not do it in front of his wife and daughter.

Hours pass by. The sun dances on the valley floor from east to west. Darker now, colder. The temperature swings in Death Valley are as wide as the valley itself.

"Take the girl upstairs." Billy looks to Victoria, who has mysteriously been making trips into the kitchen; perhaps it is a way of divorcing herself from this crime. Killing Freddy and Sam was justifiable, but this is not. Victoria's legs almost give out when she walks over to the daughter. She takes her by her arm and leads her upstairs. The wheels in her mind are starting to turn, and she might be able to get this girl out of the house.

Gio stood the whole time and kept the rifle pointed at each family member. He motions with the rifle for Maria to stand. She does. He leads her out of the house onto the front porch. Gio closes the door behind him.

"We're going to take a walk a little way from the house," Gio says while pointing the rifle at the back of Maria's head as she walks.

"What are you going to do?" Maria asks.

"Just going to take a walk. You wouldn't want to see it, would you?"

"See what?"

"Your husband killed."

Maria stops walking. She closes her eyes and begins to weep. Her head tilts up to see the stars in the night sky. She knows it will be the last time she sees them.

Billy is left in the empty living room with Martin. There is a stillness in the room. A quiet sort of acceptance overtakes Martin. He wishes a cavalry of police would burst through the door, but they won't. His thoughts shift to the first time he met his wife. It was twenty-two years ago, and he was a farmhand on the outskirts of Death Valley. Martin had been replacing shingles on a farmhouse in the town of Shoshone and tripped himself coming down a ladder. A visit to the local clinic for treatment is where he met a young nurse named Maria Deere. Once he locked in on her hazel eyes, he knew she was the woman for him. Six years later came their only child, Summer. She was now upstairs, held hostage by that strange girl this man in front of him was with.

Martin decides at this moment. He will not die without a fight. His hands are tied, but his feet are not. In a flash, he bolts up, charges at Billy, and buries his head into Billy's chest. They both crash into a wall making the entire house shake. Martin has knocked the wind out of Billy, who drops the machete.

Upstairs is Summer. She sits on the floor with her hands tied while she and Victoria listen to the struggle downstairs. Summer is in shock. Her face is pale, and her mouth is open to bringing in whatever air she can get. Victoria looks out of the bedroom window and can see Gio pointing the rifle at the back of the mother's head. Victoria picks up summer by her tied wrists and takes her to the bedroom window. She starts to untie Summer's hands.

"You need to go. Jump out this window and run." Victoria is struggling with the knots as Summer stares at her blankly. Another crash from downstairs makes the girls jump.

Billy is strong, but Martin is built like a plow horse. He uses his shoulders and head like a battering ram to wear Billy down. All four walls are caved in, and the wood frame underneath is being exposed. Martin backs up at the opposite end of the living to deliver a heavy running blow. He can also feel the rope around his wrists beginning to loosen. Billy is trying to catch his breath from the several broken ribs he now has. He spots the machete in the middle of the room.

Outside, Maria has turned to face the house. She can hear the fight inside.

"You won't shoot me. You would have done it by now. Take our truck and leave. Let me help my family. Please, untie me." Maria takes a step towards Gio.

"Don't fucking move! I will shoot!"

"Please. My daughter. She is my world. I need to see her. Just take the truck and leave." Maria pleads with her tied wrists outstretched. She takes another step, and there is a flash of white light and an intense pressure that hits her forehead that lasts only a millisecond. Gio has shot Maria, and she drops instantly. The back of her head has been blasted out, and her blood and brains seep into the dry soil of the valley.

The blast from the rifle outside stops Martin in his tracks. He looks to his right at the front door. His hands are free, and he forgets about Billy only for a brief moment and thinks of his wife. Billy seizes the moment and goes for the machete. When Martin looks back to Billy, he sees the blade going from his left to right under his chin. He goes to charge Billy but stops. He can't breathe. He feels the wet warm flow come down his chest. He grabs his throat and can feel the pulse of blood ejecting from a massive wound. Martin falls to his knees and chokes on his own blood. Before he dies, his final thought is of his daughter upstairs alone and scared and possibly dead or dying herself. Billy watches and hears his last few gurgled breaths.

Gio is looking down at the body of Maria. There is a small sense of regret in him. *Take the truck. Get to the Buick. Get the money in the trunk. Then get your ass to Mexico.* The plan is simple, and it isn't because the plan involves him abandoning Billy. Gio knows they can't stay here now. Police will be looking for them. It's not a matter of if they get caught, but when. *Take the truck and go.* Gio thinks about it, and he does it.

Billy is gathering himself from his injuries when he hears the engine from the truck outside kick over. He goes to the front door and opens it to see the red tail lights of the truck get smaller and smaller and more obscured by the dust kicking up. The disappointment he feels is great. Everything he's worked for is slipping away. All that is left is Victoria and the girl upstairs. If he can convince Victoria to continue with him, all of this won't be in vain. To do that, he must follow through and show her his dedication. Billy walks over to Martin's body and passes the kitchen door. He doesn't notice the kitchen telephone receiver being off the hook. The emergency dispatcher is listening quietly on the other end of the phone. Victoria called them before taking Summer upstairs.

Summer's hands are free, and the window is open on the second story. Victoria pleads with her to jump, but Summer doesn't want to leave her parents. To her, there is a chance they are still alive. Another reason holding her back is fear. The outside is now cold and dark, but the inside is familiar. Summer's mind is clouded as she hears heavy footsteps coming up the stairs.

"He's coming. You have to go." Victoria is whispering. She cannot get through to this girl. She sees the girl wearing a cheap gold necklace with the name "Summer" on it. She takes a chance that this is her name.

"Summer, you need to go. He will kill you." Victoria holds eye contact, and finally, the fog Summer is in begins to lift. She puts her left hand on the window sill and lifts her right foot when the bedroom door opens. Billy stands in the doorway with the machete in his right hand. His eyes go to Victoria, who pins herself against the wall. Her eyes go down to the rope on the floor. Billy's eyes go there too. Summer tries to get her foot up on the window sill to jump, but Billy's voice stops her cold.

"Stop!" Billy walks to Summer. She turns to Billy and watches him come to her. He is covered in sweat, bruises and blood. Some of the blood is her father's. He drops the machete.

Victoria is pinned by the window. He puts his right hand on Summer's face. This is the opportunity Billy has been waiting for. He can now show Victoria how far he is willing to go. All they have been through is leading to something bigger than either of them. The doubt will vanish after this, and her devotion to him will be complete.

"You will be my first." Billy looks deep into Summer's eyes. He pulls her body into him for an embrace. She doesn't bother to fight. She is small, and Billy is strong. She can feel his chest muscles against her body. Summer doesn't know if she is going to be kidnapped or killed. Billy looks up to the ceiling, opens his mouth, and buries his teeth into the left side of her neck in one quick move. She winces from the pressure, and her left arm goes numb. She can hear and feel crunching in her neck as arteries, muscles and tendons are chewed. A ravenous sound comes from Billy, and Summer goes limp in his arms as the blood exits her furiously.

Victoria is nauseous and turns to the cool wind coming in through the open window. She doesn't hesitate and jumps. She lands hard but is full of adrenaline. She gets up and runs somewhere, anywhere, with a hairline crack in her left ankle.

Billy is in ecstasy and does not see Victoria's jump. He finally pulls away from the large and monstrous wound in Summer's neck. Her lifeless body falls harshly on the wood floor. Billy has completed his ascension. Billy is now what he always wanted to be. Billy Mallek has become a vampire. Billy opens his eyes and looks around the room. He doesn't see Victoria, and that fills him with panic.

"Victoria!" Billy shouts. He goes to the window. *Did she jump? How could she leave?* His mind is rattled, and his ferocity becomes boundless. His entire dream shattered. Victoria has abandoned him.

"Victoria!" Billy shouts at the top of his lungs, goes for the window, and looks out at the empty cold farmland below. His mouth is full of blood, and the wind from the valley carries the sound of sirens. He looks up to see the flashing red and blue lights of police dancing on the faces of the mountain range. They're close. Billy hurries downstairs and out the front door of the farmhouse. He runs in the direction he came. He is running to the Buick parked two miles south.

Navigated by moonlight, Billy traverses through the winding trails. He has lost track of time. He walks and walks, but he can't come up with a plan. Victoria and Gio deserted him. His plans for a commune of his own were now all but destroyed. Victoria was not a witness to his ascension because she became frightened and fled. Up ahead, Billy finds the car. Tracks from the Chuska's truck are in the dirt near it. The trunk of the Buick is open, and he immediately knows Gio has taken the money hidden under the spare tire and driven off in the family's truck.

Billy slams the trunk shut and gets behind the wheel. The keys were left in the ignition in case the need for a quick getaway. Billy keeps the headlights off and steers the car cautiously through the valley. At any moment, he expects to see police cars. He doesn't look for Victoria. He imagines that she has already been picked up and is telling the police everything while being put in handcuffs. Billy assumes Gio is headed to Mexico, as he has wanted to do since the first killings. Using the North Star as a guide, Billy is driving east. If he can cross over the back into Nevada, he can swap out the car. Death Valley is too large and sparsely populated for that. The last thing Billy wants is to be looking for a car to steal; he just needs to see one to steal.

Billy gets to Death Valley Junction and gets on Route 127. The darkness is like a blanket and gives Billy a sense of security. He goes right, then left on State Line Road, which leads back to Nevada. Thirty seconds pass, and Billy's heart jumps. Red and Blue lights flood the inside of his black Buick Regal, and he instinctively slams his foot down on the accelerator. In this wide-open country with little to no traffic, Billy's car is no match for a police cruiser. A police cruiser is designed specifically for high-speed pursuits. They have better handling, cooling systems, and more horsepower with eight-cylinder engines. The only chance Billy has is to keep his light off and hope for oncoming traffic to keep the police from overtaking him. Over the next few miles, Billy is going at a top speed of 80 miles per hour. The cruiser is on his bumper. The cop is debating sending the Buick into a fishtail. One oncoming pedestrian car did pass, so he was apprehensive about the maneuver.

When in pursuit of a speeding vehicle, there are no jurisdiction laws. State Line Road is now Bell Vista Road. Over the California border back into Nevada, the cruiser is on Billy. In a quick bump to the left rear tire, the Buick does begin to fishtail, and the Buick does a complete 180-degree turn. Billy slams the brakes, and the cruiser stops front bumper to front bumper. The rookie officer feels the pursuit is over and exits his vehicle. Billy sees the portly Latino officer with a crew cut exit the car with sidearm drawn.

"Out of the car now!"

Billy already has the gear in reverse and hits the accelerator. The rookie officer fumbles, putting his sidearm back in his holster and jumps back into his cruiser. Billy has bought himself a few extra seconds but does not turn the car around. He is driving in reverse with the lights off. There is a fork in the road ahead. South Spring Meadows Road connects with Bell Vista Road.

A white eighteen-wheeler is heading south and getting ready to merge onto Bell Vista Road. It is a "Guaranteed Overnight Delivery" truck that has dropped off its load at a nearby chemical facility. To stay awake, the trucker changes his CB radio frequency to see if he can find a warm body at a truck stop in California. Up ahead to his right are the red and blue lights of the police car, but the trucker hasn't noticed. When he merges onto Bell Vista Road, he catches the flashing lights to his right and uses both feet to brake. A loud terrible crash sends him up and out of his seat.

The rookie officer suddenly sees a pair of headlights over the hood of the blacked-out Buick. He swerves off the road and into a ditch. As his tires screech off the blacktop, he can hear the terrible crash.

Billy's mouth was full of blood, and his head was full of anger. He wasn't ready to die but could accept it if it happened. As he flew down Bell Vista in reverse, his eyes were sore from the flashing red and blue lights coming toward him. The inside of his Buick filled with white light from behind, and the terrible sound of tires shrieking was the last thing ever to be imprinted in his brain. The sound was of metal smashing, twisting and folding around him and a terrible high-tone pitch as his head and body were pulverized by the grill of an eighteen-wheeler.

The trucker has since staggered out to see the twisted fiery metal intertwined with the front of his truck.

"I didn't see him!" The trucker says to the officer coming up out of the ditch. The rookie officer has made it to the scene, a little shaken. He puts his hands on his knees and motions to the trucker to get away from the fire.

"Get away! Get away!" The officer keeps twenty feet from the crash and can see the charred body in the front seat. A metal pipe protrudes through the center left of the chest, almost like a stake through a vampire's heart. He walks to the side of the eighteen-wheeler and stands next to the truck driver. He cocks his head and sees the large, black lettering on the side of the truck. "Guaranteed Overnight Delivery" or G.O.D.

Chapter 22

Following Day

June, 1998

A Night's Inn is located seventy miles west of Death Valley in Ridgecrest, California. It is a rust-colored one-level motel. Exiting room 13 is Gio. He is showered, shaved and wearing new clothes. He slings a backpack over his shoulder and heads south on foot. He hopes to make it to a truck stop this morning and tip generously for a ride over the border into Mexico. The money is not in his backpack. It is taped around his legs and waist. He is fluent in Spanish, and his plan is straightforward. Find a room, hit a brothel, charm a girl and stay with her. He then must find a dentist to only hide his vile teeth with dentures. After that, he must find a place, preferably near a tourist town. He can steal and manipulate tourists and slip back into the faces of the locals in Cancun or Cozumel.

To make a living as a criminal in Mexico is easy for locals, but for an American is near impossible. Criminals can spot other criminals. Gio will have to avoid not only detection by authorities but also a bullet from the competition. After some time, he cut his teeth in the Mexican underworld. In the following years, rumors began of a drug syndicate rising out of central Mexico called "Los Vampiros." Their leader was fluent in both Spanish and English. His smile is grotesque, and his greed for power is unmatched. Giovanni Gomez was a high school dropout from New Jersey, but he will be on the F.B.I.'s ten most wanted list in the coming years. That is a story for another time.

Just as Gio was crossing into Mexico for the first time, Victoria was looking to rest. She had hitchhiked back to Nevada in the wee hours of the morning. She had no money, so she had to rely on the kindness of strangers to get as far as she had. She got to Indian Springs Park in Nevada and rested on the bleachers by a baseball field. She closed her eyes and dreamed of Billy. She dreamt of better times with him. In her dreams, they were not fugitives, they were not damaged, they were not poor, and they were only in love. She then dreams of Summer Chuska with her back to Victoria. Her hair is long, and gold and white light bathe her. She slowly turns and looks at Victoria and smiles. She has fangs, and her eyes turn black. Summer rushes to Victoria with her mouth open and grabs her shoulders. Victoria awakens from her dream to a police officer grabbing her shoulder.

"Victoria Black, you are under arrest." The officer recites to Victoria her rights. She half-expected this and did not pay attention to the officer. She only feels a hole in her stomach. The hole is akin to a lost opportunity or opportunity. She regrets not trying to stop Billy or at least trying harder at any point during these past few weeks. He was just too far gone and blinded by some force. He needed to be greater than he was and show her that he was who he, in fact, said he was. A vampire.

"Do you understand the rights I have just read to you?" Asks the officer while handcuffing Victoria.

"Yes. Can I ask you a question?"

"One."

"Do you have any food?"

Victoria Black would spend the next fifteen years in prison on various charges. Since she did not technically commit any acts of murder, she was charged with conspiracy, theft, and aiding and abetting. She would later relocate to Orlando, Florida.

Chapter 23

One week later

June, 1998

She was lying down in the dying light. She raised her right hand and saw in horror her hand was almost skeletal. The light from the battery-powered lantern begins to fade. In the right corner of the room were boxes of bottled water, batteries, twelve cans of dried fruit and toilet paper. In the left corner of the room was a mattress. The lower right corner of the room was clean and had a tiny beam of sunlight that would shine through a pipe in the roof. The lower left corner of the room was her makeshift bathroom. Since the cans of dried food have been eaten, she has not had any food in six days. She has been eating pieces of cardboard from the box the batteries were kept in. This ten-by-ten metal room was meant as a temporary punishment by Freddy Bile. The intention was reprogramming so this woman would be loyal and see the error in her ways. She had come to the realization that Freddy must be dead after the third week. Too long has this punishment lasted. There were no visits, no clues, no instructions. The first week she yelled, her voice hoarse and would bang on the metal walls hoping someone above would hear. The second week she behaved and kept quiet. In the third week, she knew something was wrong and that she was trapped indefinitely, if not forever. After the fourth week, she just waited to die.

A rustling is heard above as leaves and sand are being crushed by something heavy. *A car? My God, could it be a car?* The woman gets up from the mattress, and her knees crack. She is too weak to scream, so she throws her body against the metal walls of her container. She will throw her body against these metal walls until her heart gives. One last push is all she has to save her life.

Up above, a police cruiser has come to a stop. James exits the vehicle and walks to the wooded area behind Pine Acres. He has just gotten word that William Mallek died two nights ago. To satisfy his curiosity, which some might call morbid, he has traveled back to Pine Acres to look around the property. He knows of the missing persons that were last seen at Pine Acres but were never found. The area behind Pine Acres is acres of pitch pines, oak trees, sand, and loose dirt. Controlled burns are done annually by the township to prevent brush fires. Pine Acres itself is in foreclosure by the bank. Toms River Township has expressed an interest in purchasing the parcel of land. Since it is designated residential, they hope to build low-cost housing on the property. James wants one last look before the bulldozers come in the next few months. He kicks the loose soil under his feet and walks in a circle. Rotted tires, plastic bottles, rusted beer cans, makeshift fire pits, and old furniture are strewn about. A thump is heard. James continues to walk in a circle. Another thump, but James pays it no mind. Toms River is not far from military bases that often set off explosives and bombs for training exercises. Locals are used to it, while people unfamiliar think there is a thunderstorm coming or war.

Something big catches James' eye. A doe is standing under a dead oak tree. A female has no antlers. The doe doesn't retreat in fright. Instead, it lowers its head and begins to sniff an orange metal pipe sticking one foot out of the ground. The paint is chipped, and the pipe is no more than six inches in circumference. James walks over, and the doe leaps into the brush behind it. James kicks the orange pipe, and there is another thump, but this thumping noise is different. The noise sounds metallic. James looks down the pipe and sees nothing, but the smell resembles sewage. He then takes his flashlight and directs the beam down the pipe as best he can while also trying to look down it. Something is moving. After each move, the metallic thump bounces up to him. James starts tapping on the exposed orange pipe with his flashlight, and the thumping becomes more rapid. He kicks away at the loose dirt and sand and begins to see more orange metal under his feet. He runs to his cruiser and calls the station for backup.

"Officer Gardener…Pine Acres…Route 37…Requesting back up…There are bodies here…People are trapped." He drops the receiver and goes back to the exposed metal. He is frantically looking for a door or a handle to pull. One more kick of dirt exposes the edge of the plywood. He kneels down and pries the plywood from the orange metal container with only his fingers. There is still too much dirt on top, and the plywood is too heavy. He gets up and kicks more dirt off and is able to wedge his fingertips under the plywood and lift. At about waist high the plywood snaps in half. James looks down into the hole and can see someone looking up at him. She is shielding her eyes from the sunlight. Her hair is matted, and her clothes are tattered.

"You're ok now! My name is Officer Gardener. Are you hurt?" Breathing heavily and covered in sweat, James reaches his arm down into the container. The woman extends her right hand, and James can see the skin is thin and tight to her face, but he knows her. She was reported missing a little over six weeks ago. James has found Angela Mallek.

Bulldozers had come, as did backhoes, trucks, and men with shovels. The area behind Pine Acres was torn up, and ten more containers were discovered. Most were empty, but some had remained in them. Police began scouring more acreage behind the property, looking for any sign of life or lack thereof. James leaned against his cruiser and watched as the crime scene unfolded and developed in front of him. He was ashamed that all this had happened under his watch. *How many screams in the night had gone unanswered?* He felt sick. Four skeletal remains were found. Too early to tell who. James assumed they were all females and drifters. One name he remembered was Rebecca Bailey from eleven years ago. She had been reported missing by her parents, and her last known whereabouts were in Toms River. He was confident she was one of the four. James looks up and sees dusk approaching. He opens the car door, slumps down behind the wheel of his police car and starts the engine. His job is done for today.

Chapter 24

July, 1998

The tears have dried on her cheeks. They are fuller now. She has put on ten pounds since being admitted to the hospital. Solid foods were difficult the first week. She will be released from the hospital in three days, and there is not much to look forward to. Angela had gotten word of Billy's death on her second day in the hospital two weeks prior. The pain is still as fresh as when she first heard the news. She also knows that he killed Freddy even though the investigation is still ongoing.

All wrong. All my decisions were wrong. Her son was dead despite acting in Billy's best interest and her own. She lies here now without any family around her. She is stronger physically than she has been in weeks, but internally, her heart and spirit are near death. The only thing keeping her alive in her makeshift metal tomb was the thought of one day reuniting with her son and making amends. Now she cannot.

All she remembers on the night of her disappearance was an accusation by Freddy that she had told Alexis about the Community. Then blackness. She recollects bits and pieces. Randy Claxton dumped boxes of food and water in her underground prison. Reassuring words that Freddy would be back to talk with her. Then nothing. Everything stopped. She was left to die. She can understand Freddy leaving her since he was dead, but the thought of Randy leaving her to die is repulsive. Freddy's and Randy's motives haunted her. The coldness of people was what she wanted to avoid. That's why she and Tasha came to New Jersey in the first place. Now she lay here alone, abandoned, and fearful of a future that is bleak at best. On the night table next to her bed on the left is a vase of yellow roses. The note was simple. "Get better soon. Thinking of you. Tasha." There was no number or address. No way for Angela to contact her. It's the thought that counts, but even that felt half-empty. It was nice to hear from Tasha, but she knew she would never visit or call. That bridge was burned. Too many things had happened. Awful things. It all could have been avoided if better choices had been made.

Angela ponders what trajectory her and her son's life would have taken if she had just stayed with Tasha. The relationship might have been kept secret for another ten years or more, but times have changed, and there is more acceptance. Billy would have never grown up with the sick influence of Freddy. There's no telling where his life would have gone. He would be alive. Angela knew that. The tears began again, but Angela could only wipe them away with her left hand. Her right hand is handcuffed to the hospital bed.

For her involvement with Freddy Bile and the Community at Pine Acres, she does face criminal charges similar to those of Victoria Black. There were human remains found on the property that Angela had managed for nearly twenty years. Law enforcement cannot look away from that despite the pain and suffering she had endured. Again, her future was bleak at best. After serving her time, Angela disappeared, and her current whereabouts are unknown.

Chapter 25

August, 1998

A barbecue is a Saturday tradition at the Gardener house in South Toms River. James sits with Clarence on the back deck, having a beer while Thomas and his parents set the table. James is surprised that his sister, Denise, is getting along with Jason's new girlfriend. Clarence has noticed that James is in better spirits. His eyes are open more, and he has even cracked a few smiles today.

"How are you feeling? Things are going better at work?" Asks Clarence.

"The same."

"You seem to be in a better mood. Ever since you saved that woman."

"Been thinking about that. Anyone would have done the same."

"But they didn't. You did. They treating you any differently down at the precinct?" Clarence takes a swig of his beer and places it on the deck. He turns his chair to face his son head-on. James knows his father wants more than just yes and no answers.

"They do. It's a strange feeling now. I think it's like vindication." James answers.

"How so?"

"Well, everyone thinks I get too obsessed over things, like a compulsive disorder. I focus on something until my head hurts. That's why I went back to Pine Acres that day. I needed time to think, focus and find more answers."

"Because you're fastidious with details, you went back. That going back is what saved that woman's life. Did you find your answers?"

"No, but that doesn't matter. If I wasn't the way I am, someone would have died. It's like I was supposed to be there. I watched the animals like you said. There was a doe there. Looked right at me as they all do, but this was different. She didn't freeze up or take off. She wanted me to see. I was meant to be right there at that exact moment."

"And you got your vindication."

"Yes." James watches Thomas with his father, and Clarence notices.

"Ever want a family of your own, James? I know I've asked you before."

"I'm open to it. When things are better in this town. A little less evil." James flashes a sarcastic, sideways smile to his father.

"Well, evil doesn't work on your time. The world will always be a little evil. A little off. You balance that out by choosing to put some good in it." Clarence adjusts his chair forward and picks up his beer. He looks out at the sky over the roof of his back neighbor's house. He knows he will have another grandson, not by his daughter, but by his son.

Chapter 26

May, 1996

Michael should be a sophomore but isn't. Algebra had bested him, and even with the aid of tutors, he failed. So here he sits as a freshman staring blankly at the blackboard with its charts and graphs. Michael could never wrap his mind around the concept that letters can equal numbers in this mathematical expression. He simply tuned out. Due to his health issues and compromised learning, he would eventually be given an exemption from his guidance counselor for algebra. Today, however, he sits quietly. Behind him is Peter Mitel. To some, Peter's head looks like it is on a swivel. Bouncing up and down and going from side to side. Never fixating on one thing. It is not that he isn't paying attention to his teacher. He is actually paying attention to everything in the room. Peter hones in on different sounds. A girl to his left is scribbling out a wrong answer, and he can hear the ballpoint pen going back and forth very hard and fast. He can hear the air conditioning kicking on through the vented grate above and to the rear of the classroom. His head turns toward a pencil dropping in the front of the room. Peter can even hear a yellow jacket wasp bouncing off the classroom window.

Peter's eye sockets are sunken in his head. He was born with anophthalmia meaning he was born without eyes. His algebra textbook is in braille. Leaning against his desk is his walking stick. Peter sits behind Michael because Michael leads him from class to class during the day. Peter has memorized all the routes to his classes, but the hallways are crowded, and he fears bumping into other kids and dropping his books. When class ends, he always grabs his stick in his left hand, places his right hand on Michael's right shoulder, and lets him lead the way.

The bell rings, and algebra is done for the day, mercifully for Michael.

"You ready?" Michael asks Peter.

"Yeah. Did you want to come over later and play Nintendo with my brother?" Peter takes his stick in his left hand and has his right hand on Michael's shoulder. Michael also carries Peter's books.

"Maybe. I have to ask my mom," says Michael.

Peter has known Michael since elementary school. He can sense that Michael doesn't have many friends, if any. Peter would overhear other students snicker and make fun of Michael and his drooping left eye. Peter didn't feel sorry for many people considering his own condition, but Michael was different. Peter related to him and did feel sorry for him.

As the two navigate the halls, Peter and Michael hear a rude comment from behind them.

"Blind leading the blind."

Michael turns to see two senior football players barreling through all the smaller kids in the hall. The two complete the look by wearing their respective football jerseys even though the season is long over. When the two seniors get next to Michael and Peter, they do take pity on Peter, but not on Michael and push him hard into the lockers dropping his and Peter's books. Since Peter was using Michael as a guide, he also lost his balance a little.

"Assholes," Peter says.

The hallway is close to empty now. Some kids laugh at Michael as he picks up the textbooks, but most have sympathy and choose not to look. Michael, of course, only hears the laughter. Michael gets up with books under his left arm and Peter's hand back on his right shoulder. With his ego bruised again, Michael mutters quietly to himself.

"One day, I'll kill them all." Michael forgets that Peter has excellent hearing and hears every word.

Chapter 27

End of August, 1998

Michael is in his work truck driving by his former high school. He can see cars pulling into the parking lot. Classes start in one week, but Michael will not be entering his senior year. It's a lazy Saturday afternoon, and the summer has been long and hot. The football team and the cheerleading squad have reported to school early for practices. Michael decides to drive into the parking lot and watch practice from his truck.

The football field is behind the school and separated from it by the parking lot. Michael parks his truck to face the football field, where the varsity football players are running scrimmages. The cheerleaders, in casual clothes, are going over their cheer routines while sneaking glances at the varsity players. The air is heavy, and the humidity is oppressive. Michael rolls down his windows to catch what little air he can. The air conditioning in the truck hasn't worked in years. Michael watches with no emotion at first. After about ten minutes, he gets a sharp pain in his chest that he recognizes as jealousy. He examines the discontent the best he can. The structure and hierarchy of it all are what bothers him. The jocks get all the advantages, preferential treatment and attention from girls. The cheerleaders also get the advantages and attention from all the boys. They can all afford to be selective and ungrateful for the attention they get because it is all so readily available to them. Arbitrary and shallow, it all seems to Michael. He assumes the worst of them, not considering or even aware of the years of work they put in. To him, they haven't earned their status, and he is unwilling to acknowledge that anyone in their position would do the same. To Michael, it is abhorrently unfair and even wicked.

A familiar and sharp pain is now in between his shoulder blades. The pain triggers something in the far reaches of his mind, and Michael seems to slip away. He begins to justify, twist and quantify certain truths learned from his haphazard religious self-education. A sort of manifesto begins to take shape. He is not staring at the football players and the cheerleaders but through them. He is looking past them into his "void." We cannot explore there because we risk not being able to come back. At least not in the same way we were before.

The coach's whistle is loud enough to wake Michael up from his trance. He has been gone for one hour. He starts his truck and drives off slowly, looking back at the football field through his rearview mirror.

A cascade of medical problems has come down on Paul since his heart attack. The first hole in a leaking dam has weakened the structure, and now different cracks and leaks begin to form. He is constantly tired, weak, forgetful and in pain. His joints, especially his hands, ache all day and night. Years of working with his hands have only helped destroy the cartilage between the bones. Now he can barely hold a pencil. Laura only visits twice a week. She was able to secure help with Paul through a hospice agency. A thick Russian woman was sent to stay with Paul from seven in the morning until seven at night. Natalia had moved to America fifteen years prior and became a citizen soon after that. Her father was a prominent physician in Omsk, and her mother was a schoolteacher. Natalia never found the men in Russia smart enough or financially stable enough to suit her needs. Most of the single men were alcoholics and made little money working in the factories. She learned English and spoke it fluently by the age of twelve. Her training in medical school in Omsk only translated to a nursing position in the United States. While furthering her studies here, she met her future husband. He was a teacher's assistant and eventually became a professor at Monmouth University. Natalia is now forty years old and feels guilty for not having children. She followed the western feminist ideals of career first and family second, if at all. Now she was apprehensive about having a child due to the increased chance of defects due to her age.

While Paul was rubbing his swollen hands on the sofa, Natalia made dinner. She was used to making a hearty stew that she had learned from her grandmother. Sausage, beef, bacon, with potatoes. With Paul's heart condition, she couldn't make anything so heavy. It was old-fashioned chicken noodles tonight. In her downtime, Natalia would read cheap American romance novels. It was the only escapism that she allowed herself. While Paul ate, she read. Tonight she couldn't concentrate on her reading because she noticed a wheezing sound coming from Paul as he ate. It was as if the ordeal of eating was too strenuous for him.

"Are you okay, Mr. Phy? You seem tired?" She asks.

"I'm fine. Been a long day. I'll go to bed after dinner. Laura will be in later to check on me and the house." Paul coughs a little and continues eating. Tomorrow Natalia will bring up the idea to Laura about taking Paul to check his lungs. She is worried about his labored breathing. Natalia didn't care much for Laura. She found her ill-tempered, bossy, and cold. Natalia, of course, had been accused of being all three by Laura herself. The two were more similar than different. However, the one difference was rather colossal. Natalia loved life, and Laura did not.

"Your son does not visit much. Why?"

"Work."

"Too busy to see his own father? Nonsense." Natalia studies Paul for any reaction.

"He finished the driveway for me. Fixed the fence in the backyard just the other day."

"That was two weeks ago. What is my name?" Natalia cocks her head to one side.

"What are you talking about?" Paul puts down his fork and sits back.

"Your son has not been here for two weeks. You got up the other day to go to work, but you are now retired. What year is it?"

"1998, Natalia." Paul gives her a sarcastic smile and goes back to his soup.

"Good." Natalia pretends to return to her book, but all the while, she is thinking of taking Paul to have his memory checked.

The next morning Natalia and Laura are in the waiting room of Doctor Solomon. Natalia is reading her romance novel while Laura is checking her watch.

"Been in there for forty minutes," Laura says while tapping her foot.

"The doctor is recommending tests. He will probably need CT and MRI scans. His mind is starting to go." Natalia tells Laura.

"He's not losing his mind. Terrible thing to say. I thought we were just checking his breathing."

"He has memory issues as well as breathing problems. He can't balance his checkbook. He pays me in cash for groceries and only gives me singles because he loses concentration with big numbers. Mr. Phy probably has early stages of Alzheimer's."

"You're not a doctor. You're only a nurse." The news is too much for Laura.

"How do you know he doesn't have Alzheimer's? You're only a cashier." Natalia one-ups Laura. Just then, the nurse pokes her head into the waiting area.

"You are with Mr. Phy, correct?"

"Yes, we both are," Laura answers.

"The doctor would like to talk with you both."

Natalia and Laura get up and follow the nurse through the small hallway into the first exam room. Paul is sitting on the examination table with his hands folded with a sour look. Doctor Solomon is standing next to Paul with a manilla folder clutched to his chest. He is tall, balding, thin, with black horn-rimmed glasses. He smiles out of courtesy to Laura and Natalia.

"Please, have a seat." Doctor Solomon then closes the door to the room very slowly, as if he is delaying the news he is about to give.

Chapter 28

Tuesday

September 8, 1998

Mr. Lundy is seventy-two years old but looks much older. He sits on his back porch,

watching Michael clear some overgrown brush from the edges of his property. After removing

the brush, Michael will power wash his plastic green-stained fence back to white. Mr. Lundy is

impressed by Michael's work ethic. The temperature is nearly ninety degrees, and Michael has

not taken a break in three hours. Like most elderly living in senior communities, family only

visits during holidays. Only when the elderly are on death's door, does the family make more of

an effort to visit? When a person like Michael shows up, it is an opportunity to socialize and get

a feel for the outside world again. That's why the only people who strike up conversations with

grocery store clerks are the elderly. Mr. Lundy spent most of his days inside, watching cable

news and lamenting a changing world. He waves for Michael to come over and sit with him on

the porch.

"Married?"

"No, I'm only eighteen."

"Girlfriend?"

"No."

"Well, there will be time for that. I was married at nineteen. Had two girls. Then I got

sent to the front lines in Korea. Haven't had your great war yet. It will come eventually. It always does. Men can't help themselves. Have to be fighting something. Make sure you don't have any internal wars, and you'll be alright. What happened to your eye?" Mr. Lundy asks with no filter.

"Born with it. Brain swelled and caused deformity in my skull."

"Well, we all have scars. It isn't very noticeable. You're a strong young man. Ever consider the military?"

"No. I can't think that far ahead."

"If you want a family of your own one day, you will need a good job. I always wanted to be a pilot, but I had lousy eyesight. Did you ever have a dream or a goal?"

"I don't dream."

"Don't be silly. Every young man dreams. That's how we got running water, cars, and airplanes. Every man dreams."

"I can't dream."

"Come inside." Mr. Lundy doesn't seem to hear Michael, and he gets up and enters his home. Michael follows behind him. The inside is dark and dusty, with a smell of mold. Mr. Lundy leads Michael into the kitchen and opens a door that has been painted over so many times that it sticks when he opens it. A quick flick of a switch and wooden stairs can be seen. The two go down into the basement. Another light switch is hit, and the fluorescent lights pop on. All four walls are covered in artillery, neatly placed and labeled in glass cabinets. The four walls house the older model rifles, shotguns and handguns. The Winchester, Remingtons, Brownings, Lugers, Colts, and Smith and Wessons are Mr. Lundy's most valued possessions.

"You can say I'm a bit of a collector. My son-in-law brings me newer models. I keep them in the center cabinet. I'm running out of room." Mr. Lundy walks to a center metal cabinet and opens the drawers. Inside are the more modern weapons with the proper ammunition set next to each piece of hardware. "Every man dreams, Michael. This was one of mine. Took the better part of forty years to get it. Some were even used in combat."

Michael walks around the room and looks into each glass cabinet. He examines each shotgun, rifle, and handgun on display. Index cards are next to each with the model number and year. His real interest is in the center metal cabinet where Mr. Lundy is. Together they look through each drawer. The handguns are in the top two drawers. The rifles are in the third and fourth. The bottom drawer has two compact assault rifles. The sleek design in each is what captures Michael's imagination. He has only seen weapons like these on television and in the movies.

"The internet is a heck of a thing." Mr. Lundy only touches the guns. He never takes them out or fires them. They are for show. They should be used. Michael can't help but feel that it is a waste.

"Why don't you use them?" Michael asks.

"On what? Deer? I don't like killing things. I just appreciate the art and craftsmanship."

Michael instinctively looks for basement windows for reasons we will never know. There are two. Michael makes a mental note.

"Now, when you get home, I want you to start thinking of your dreams and what you want out of life. Will you do that?" Mr. Lundy closes up the drawers. Michael only nods with a smile that sends a surprising shiver up Mr. Lundy's spine. *Something's off with him. No dreams.*

"Alright then. Let's finish up the yard." Mr. Lundy gathers himself and motions to the door with his eyes. He makes sure to be the last to leave the room. He doesn't want Michael behind him.

After finishing work, Michael drives to a local department store. He needs to buy motor oil to finish a job for one of his father's customers. Michael has been indifferent to his father's recent diagnosis. Paul is in the early stages of dementia, and his nurse, Natalia, pesters Michael to come inside and spend time with his father. He never did before, so he doesn't see the purpose of doing it now.

While going to the automotive section of the store, Michael sees Halloween decorations already up. Besides Christmas, Halloween is the second most popular holiday in America and is only considered one because of retail. It is a consumer-based holiday like Valentine's Day, Mother's Day and Father's Day. Tens of millions are spent on candy, decorations, and costumes. On a whim, he looks at the costumes and masks. Michael was never allowed to go trick-or-treating as a child. Laura would not allow it. The excuses ranged from having to work, candy being rotten for his teeth, and her not being responsible if he ended up being hit by a car crossing the street. One mask, in particular, makes him stop. It is a very detailed latex mask of a human skull. By a strange coincidence, the mold used to make the mask had a defect in the left eye socket, making it droop just a few millimeters. Michael doesn't believe in coincidences. He picks up the mask from the rack and stares into it. A mother with her child is in the same aisle. The mother is uncomfortable in Michael's presence as he stares at this rubber skull mask. She takes her child by the hand and leaves the aisle. Michael takes the mask with him.

Michael has just finished replacing an oil filter on Paul's driveway for his father's customer. Michael wipes his hands down with a dirty rag and looks toward the back of the house. He can see Natalia watching him through the kitchen window. Michael decides to go inside. Natalia is making dinner and watches Michael enter. From the moment she met him, she knew something was off about him. His eye was not the reason. He never looks her or anyone in the eye, and his posture is always slumped. He shuffles his feet and is as awkward socially as he is physical. His one-word answers also put her on edge. He puts no effort into looking his best or even trying, which troubles Natalia the most. Michael doesn't seem to try or care about anything.

"You should say hello to your father, Michael."

"I will."

"He's in the living room." Natalia motions towards the living room. She watches him leave the kitchen and thinks about what type of person Michael will be. Her first guess is that he will not live a long life.

Michael sees Paul watching a baseball game. Paul is looking at the television but not registering what he is seeing. The players on the Yankees are unfamiliar to him. When Michael sits next to him, his first reaction is a simple greeting.

"How are you?" Asks Paul.

"Same. Has mom been around?"

"She was here this morning. She's at work now."

Michael knows that isn't true. His mother works mornings, not afternoons or evenings. He knows his father's mind and memory are deteriorating.

"She might stop by later," Michael says.

"Who is in the kitchen?"

"Your nurse."

"Nurse? I'm not sick."

"You were. Heart attack. She helps when mom isn't here."

"Heart attack?" Paul asks. His attention turns to the television and the players he does not know.

"She was here this morning. She's at work now." Paul repeats.

Before Michael enters the apartment he shares with his mother, Michael thinks about how much time his father has left. He wanted to take away his father's suffering. Being stuck at the same time for the rest of one's life is no way to live.

Michael walks through the apartment and can hear his mother mumbling and banging drawers in the kitchen. He does not talk to his mother much and usually goes directly to his room to read. This time was different. He stood in the doorway of the kitchen and watched his mother.

"Never any pens in this house! What did you do? Use them all up?!"

"No."

"Never any pens!"

"Are you going to see dad?" Michael asks.

"What for?! To watch him dribble all over himself?!" Laura continues opening and closing drawers furiously. "No pens with ink in this house!"

Michael interprets what his mother says differently. He thinks she said, "No men with dicks in this house!" Michael feels a shot of anger, and the blood rushes to his head. He will no longer be emasculated or put down by anyone, including his mother. His eyes now dart to the phone line on the baseboard of the kitchen. He goes for it and yanks it from the wall. The phone topples over and makes a terrible crashing sound. Laura turns to see what Michael is doing, and it does not register.

"What the hell are you doing?!"

Micheal wraps the phone line around his hands and lunges to his mother. He wraps the line around her neck. Laura's glasses come off, and she starts kicking in the air as Michael lifts her off the floor. She clips the kitchen table with her foot and almost tips it over. Michael spins her around and around with the line around her throat tightening. Laura reaches behind her and can only scratch at her son's face. Michael is far too strong, and Laura can feel the bones in her neck breaking and the arteries in her neck constricting. There is no air anymore, and there are no words or screams, only muffled gags. The veins in her temples begin to burst, as do the capillaries in her eyes. She eventually stops fighting. There were no last thoughts, only the instinct to survive and fend off the attack. Michael continues to squeeze long after Laura is dead. Her left eye has popped from its socket and is only held in place by her upper and lower eyelids. Michael lays her on the cold linoleum tile of the kitchen floor. He sees her left eye and chuckles. He takes the tablecloth from the disheveled kitchen table and drapes it over his mother's body. He stands over her and breathes heavily. The apartment is quiet. Michael can hear children playing outside. A shaft of sunlight pierces into the kitchen and lands on his mother's covered face. There is a tap on the kitchen window. Michael looks to see a wasp confused by its reflection bouncing off it. Michael takes his keys from his work truck out of his pocket and leaves the kitchen. He goes to his bedroom and takes out a bag from his closet. He then leaves the apartment he once shared with his mother for the last time.

Night now, and Michael has parked his work truck under a tree and across the street from Mr. Lundy's house. He is here for one reason, the newer-model guns in the basement. He hurriedly walks across the street and onto Lundy's lawn. On the side of the house, he sees the two basement windows. A little pane of glass won't stop him. Michael takes out his serrated knife he got from Billy Mallek and cuts around the caulked edges of the glass. He pushes until the glass is free from the frame and falls silent on the carpeted basement floor. He goes in headfirst and can balance himself enough on a shelf to enter. Michael goes to the center metal cabinet and removes the guns and ammunition he wants. Each gun has its own case, so it is easy for him to simply put each case outside the basement window one by one. He removes five guns and stands on the shelf by the basement window to leave. For a moment, he contemplates using the one gallon of gasoline he has in a gas can to light Mr. Lundy's basement on fire, but he decides against it. The main objective is tomorrow; he cannot afford to get sidetracked. Michael gathers the five guns in a green army sack and heads to his truck. The only sound tonight is crickets. A sort of calm before a storm, but this storm will not be brought by nature.

Chapter 29

September 9, 1998

Wednesday, 9:55 a.m.

A police photographer is taking shots of Laura Krueger's body. The tablecloth has been removed. One of the two forensic detectives is dusting for prints while the other gathers the phone cord in an evidence bag. James is in Michael's bedroom. He is wearing latex gloves and turning the pages in Michael's bible with a pencil eraser. James can immediately tell that Michael is not a Catholic. Pages have been ripped out, passages highlighted in yellow and crude drawings of torture in the margins. "The Book of Revelation" section gives James pause. Written in pen at the top is "fifth horseman Wickedness."*Does he now see himself as a bringer of the apocalypse? From arson to murder to what? Destruction on a massive scale. Where is he going?* James' thoughts are circling. One thing he does know is that Michael is not here. He is out there somewhere, and he must be stopped.

"You chose way number two, Michael," James says to himself. He gets up and leaves the bedroom. He walks past the other detectives and officers until he is outside. He can see Michael's father sitting in an ambulance with an oxygen mask on. Natalia is next to him, helping him breathe. Natalia had come to the apartment earlier in the morning when the phone line was constantly busy. When no one answered the door, she peeked into the kitchen window and saw a body covered in a cloth. Paul had fainted when word came down that it was Laura's body. She then called the police.

James gets to his squad car and drives slowly through the apartment parking lot past the onlookers. He is not sure where he is going. He hopes it will just come to him. *The church? Shopping center? The school? Where are you?* James drives, hoping to find a sign of life or death.

The night before, Michael also drove around. After killing his mother and stealing the guns from Mr. Lundy, Michael parked his work truck on a dirt road. On his right was a fenced-in power generator. The low-frequency hum it gave off helped Michael to sleep, if only for an hour. His bag of guns, a black hooded sweatshirt, and the skull mask he bought were on the passenger seat. All Michael thought of that night was the next day. He never thought of his mother. He did think of his father, however. After he took the guns, he parked in front of his father's house. He was first going to kill Natalia, then kill his father. Not because he was angry with him, but quite the opposite. He felt terrible about his father's condition and wanted to alleviate his suffering. He wanted to make it quick. One bullet to the brain. While he sat in the truck on his father's street, contemplating how to enter the house, a police car went by. Michael got cold feet. Everything was leading to Wednesday. The day of his former high school's Pep Rally. He had come too far to be picked up, so he left his father's street and parked here for the night. He slept but did not dream by the hum of a generator.

John Healy is sixty years old and works for the maintenance department of Toms River Regional Schools. Wednesday at noon, he routinely checks the high school's backup generator in a wooded area behind the football field. It is only accessible by a gravelly dirt road. Energy use during the first week of school, combined with higher-than-normal temperatures, prompts John to make sure the generator is functioning in case of a brownout or blackout in the area. John enjoys the work and allows himself a cigar when working outside. He stops his maintenance truck on the road when he sees an old, white pickup truck parked by the generator. As he approaches from behind, John can see someone sitting in the driver's seat.

"Excuse me, are you supposed to be parked here? No one is allowed on school property." John tosses his cigar on the ground as he gets to the driver's side window.

"You can't park here." John looks at the driver. The greasy brown hair, pale skin, and deformed left eye trigger a memory. "You look familiar. What's your name?"

"Michael."

"Last name."

"Phy."

"I know you. You used to go to this school. You got kicked out. They thought you were going to burn the place down. I suggest you go, son. Don't make me call the cops. Just go." John steps back as Michael opens the driver's side door and exits. He stands in front of John, who is shorter, but thicker and barrel-chested.

"Pep Rally is today. Can't wait." Michael has his right hand in his back pocket and a grip on the handle of his pocket knife. John's eyes size Michael up, but he gets distracted for a brief, fateful second when a crow above lets out a caw.

James is in his cruiser and headed west on Bay Avenue. The high school is on his left. The new school year started yesterday, and traffic is heavy as school buses pile into the parking lot. Today is the annual Pep Rally to usher in the new football season. James has circled the school twice now. Nothing seems out of the ordinary until he looks up and sees a powerline across Bay Avenue that connects to a utility pole on school property. A murder of crows has gathered and sits on the powerlines. Hundreds of them. Crows are often associated with death because they are scavengers. Some people see them as omens of death and only gather in large numbers when something or someone is about to die. James remembers his father's words.

"Watch the animals." He quietly says as he turns into the school parking lot.

The first week of school is usually half days. Today the three thousand students will stay later to watch the rally in the gymnasium at one in the afternoon. It is now a quarter of. James navigates through the buses, faculty cars, and students' cars. He parks by the blue metal gymnasium doors. Blue and yellow are the school colors. He steps out of his cruiser and looks around. Kids go into school through the entrance. Buses are parked, and bus drivers are talking to one another in the lot. The school security guard is placing traffic cones. Nothing unusual until a single crow swoops down and flies towards the football field. James watches as the single crow meets up with another two dozen crows circling over the wooded area behind the field. A gravelly dirt road next to the field that leads to the woods is calling James. *Stay here or take the road? Those birds are circling something. Check it out and then get back here. Be fast. Go now.* James does.

John Healy is near death. The serrated blade is stuck in his neck as he drags himself to the ground. He is trying to make his way back to his truck to radio for help. He cannot speak because the blade has pierced his windpipe, and he is swallowing his own blood. He must try to signal for help somehow. If he is unable to speak, he will use his car horn. Using adrenaline and the desire to see his wife, children, and two grandsons again, he can get to his truck. He glances at his reflection in the rearview mirror and sees his face almost completely drained of blood. He grabs his radio and attempts to call back to the office, but he can't speak. He tosses the radio down in frustration and lays on his car horn.

With his sidearm drawn, James hears the car horn and rushes to the maintenance truck. When he sees John Healy covered in blood and with a knife in his neck, he immediately gets on his radio clipped to his shoulder.

"Emergency ambulance needed at Toms River High School North. Access the road behind the football field. Repeat. Emergency ambulance is needed. Requesting back up!" James sees an extra work shirt in the passenger seat of Healy's truck and grabs it. He wraps it around Healy's wound.

"Lay down across the seat. Help is coming. Keep pressure on it."

John Healy has only a little strength left, and shock is beginning to set in. He lifts his right hand and points towards the school.

"Don't move. Stay still." James says.

Healy points more emphatically toward the school. James' eyes widened. He now realizes what this man is doing. The attacker is headed towards the school. James bolts from the truck and looks toward the school, a football field away. A second maintenance truck approaches. James flags it down and talks to the shocked driver.

"Stay with that man! He's injured! Help is on the way!" James draws his sidearm again and rushes down the gravel road toward the school.

John Healy is fading in and out of consciousness. He sees his friend and co-worker Brian Dugan over him and pressing down on the wound. John has known Brian for twenty-five years. They are fishing buddies, and their families sometimes vacation together at the Jersey shore. John knows he will die by the look on Brian's face. Tears have welled up, and Brian's face is flushed.

"Stay with me. They're coming, John. I can see them. Just don't close your eyes."

John wishes he could keep his eyes open, but his eyelids weigh so much now. All he wants to do is sleep. The black is starting to encircle his vision. The blade is so deep in his neck that the slightest movement brings pain unlike any he has ever felt. He closes his eyes and can

hear Brian's fading voice telling him to stay awake. The final image he has is of a scrawny,

brown-haired boy with a sagging left eye swinging hard at his neck. *That bastard killed me.*

Chapter 30

Same Day

11:57 a.m.

After stabbing the maintenance man, Michael took the sack from his truck and swung another bag filled with guns over his shoulder. He walked fast but not too fast to draw attention. The back entrance to the school with its blue metal doors is in sight. He enters the school, and the halls are empty. Students and faculty are on the other end of the hallway entering the gymnasium for the rally. Michael enters the boy's lavatory up ahead to the right. It's quiet and empty inside. He locks the bathroom door behind him and takes the furthest stall. The bag with the guns is the heaviest, so he puts that down, and it lands with a thunk.

Michael opens the other bag and pulls out his black hooded sweatshirt. He puts it on and goes back into the bag for a can of grease. He swiped it from his father's garage the previous day. Michael takes a bit of grease from the can and makes dark circles around his eyes. Into the bag again, he takes out black leather gloves and the Halloween mask of the skull. He puts the gloves on first to not get grease on the mask. The mask is slipped on over his head, as is the black hood. He leans against the tiled wall for a moment and goes to the bag of guns. He takes out a semi-automatic rifle. He holds it. All the weapons have been preloaded, and it takes a moment for Michael to catch his breath and go over the plan in his mind for the last time. He takes the bag of guns and slings it over his right shoulder. Michael exits the stall and looks at his reflection in the cracked bathroom mirror.

Michael Anthony Phy is no more. He slipped away the moment the Fifth Horseman of the Apocalypse named Wickedness stared back at his reflection. The opportunity to fulfill his demented legacy is before him on a grand scale. Horsemen must punish the wicked. The wicked who shunned and tormented his former identity. He goes to the door and unlocks it. He enters the hallway and can hear the thousands of students gathered in the gym. They are cheering and stomping their feet on the wooden bleachers. The riotous sounds grow louder as the Horseman draws nearer with weapon in hand.

In the early 1920's Sigmund Freud, the father of psychoanalysis came out with his Personality Theory. In his theory, the human mind has three facets that make up personality. The id, the superego and the ego. The id is the most primitive of the human mind. It contains all our survival instincts with no regard for societal norms and law. The superego contains our values and morals taught by our parents, schools and church. The ego is what we consciously project to others after we have balanced out our unconscious id and superego. Michael's superego was corrupted by a poor upbringing and his self-instilled haphazard morals. His id was for too long suppressed. His ego is not strong enough to balance out the id and superego. The result is an armed psychopath walking down the hallway of a school.

James gets to the blue metal doors. He questions whether or not he should wait for his backup. He is wearing his bulletproof vest but knows he won't do any good against an assault rifle or a lucky shot to the head. He opens the door cautiously and enters. He braces the metal door behind him so it won't make a sound. Each step down the hall is like going through a minefield. He, too, can hear the pep rally starting. A creaking sound is heard to his right. James quickly presses himself against the lockers on his right. He sees the back of a man dressed in black with a bag over his right shoulder. He seems to be carrying a weapon and is walking towards the gymnasium doors up ahead.

"Freeze! Drop your weapon and turn around!" James is covered in sweat as he yells the instructions. The man in black doesn't seem to miss a beat and keeps going.

"Stop! Michael! Stop!" He fires one warning shot over the man's head, but the man doesn't stop.

"Horseman!" James shouts. James remembers the margins of the bible in Michael's room.

The man stops. He turns slowly to face the officer who has identified him. James sees the terrible mask and the hood, and the semi-automatic rifle in his hands. His heart is pounding so loud that he can't hear his own voice.

"Drop the weapon now!" James has his gun aimed at the Horseman's head, who is thirty feet ahead of him.

Horseman must pass one more obstacle before realizing and achieving his purpose. He is impressed with this officer whose face is familiar to him. *How does he know who I am?* He wants to ask him, but he is losing time and decides to kill him. Horseman pulls the trigger and begins firing. He fires in a spray pattern from right to left, but it's sloppy. Michael had never fired a gun before today. James is laser-focused and only takes two shots to bring down the Horseman. One shot to the chest and one to the head. As Horseman fell back, his firing went up and hit a sprinkler. It triggers all the other sprinklers, and the fire alarm sounds. James knows the halls will fill with students and teachers, so he stands over the Horseman's body. James looks down and into the Horseman's open eyes, particularly the left one.

The first people in the hallway are two female teachers who scream and cover their mouths. James puts away his sidearm and tells the women he is a police officer and that the situation is resolved. He instructs the two women to grab the student-made signs for the rally and make a shield around the body so the students won't see. They do, but some of the kids caught a glimpse, and they ran in fear or screamed. Other students mill about in confusion, thinking a fire has broken out and aren't sure why a cop and two teachers are obscuring their view of someone on the floor. When they see a pool of blood and water growing around the feet of the three adults, they stop and stare.

"Go on! Get out of here! Get everyone out!" James demands.

Other faculty come out and begin directing the students to the exits. One student is lost and scared. He keeps bumping into other students who are also lost and scared. Peter Mitel has lost his walking stick in the commotion. No one is leading him out to safety. All the blind can do in this situation is feel around for something familiar, like a window or a piece of furniture, but all he feels are other bodies bumping him around. Patricia Azzolini, who served detention once with Michael, sees Peter struggling. She grabs his right hand and puts it on her shoulder. Her glasses are wet, so she takes them off, wipes them on her shirt and puts them back on.

"Follow me, Peter. It's okay. We're going outside!" Patricia leads Peter away.

James watches them, and it warms him in the cold water pouring down on him, the teachers and the body of Michael Anthony Phy for a brief moment.

Chapter 31

September 14, 1998

The funeral for John Healy was heavily attended. He was well-liked in town and had a big family. His wife and children weep in the front rows of St. Joseph Church. In the back of the church in a suit is James. He wanted to attend the funeral only for a moment to pay his respects. He had spent his last few moments alive with the deceased, and it bonded them somehow. James couldn't understand why it bonded them, but it did. Maybe everything doesn't need to have an answer. The funeral for Laura Krueger was two days ago. It was held at the funeral parlor for Paul, Natalia, and a few friends from the grocery store where she worked. Laura had no living family, and her son was now also dead. Michael did not have a funeral and was buried in Riverside Cemetery with no headstone. The funeral home furnished a small metal plate with his name, date of birth and date of death. Paul and Natalia did not visit his gravesite.

James leaves John Healy's funeral early and goes outside. He leans himself against the brickwork of the church and thinks. Overhead the sky is turning dark as a storm is brewing. James does not feel angst. For the first time leaving the church, he feels relief as he breathes the late summer, early autumn air. He thinks of the soul. *What is it? What is a soul made of? Where does it go when the body is no more?* James then thinks of the souls of Billy Mallek and Michael Phy. *Where are they now?* Thunder rumbles in the distance, and James begins the walk to his car.

Chapter 32

Hell

Day of Wrath

The three have been chasing for some time now. Days are not distinguishable here. A perpetual sort of sunless dusk is the only illumination over the rocky and ragged canyons at the foothills of enormous mountains and volcanoes. The sky is red with no clouds, and the air is thick with a scent of sulfur. Distant screams, the eruptions of lava from mountaintops and the footsteps of the three are the only sounds here. When describing the three hunting, we have to merely go by the physical because their origins are unknowable. They are nude with distended bellies. Their skin is rust-colored, and their eyes are yellow. Their faces are ugly yet human. They are of differing heights, weights and strengths. No sex organs are visible, so gender is irrelevant. One can assume they are old because they have memorized the entire terrain here. There are no words spoken between them, only grunts and gestures. The three have been hunting the Vampire for a while and are getting impatient. They are impressed by his speed and cunning. Their motive for hunting the Vampire is known only to them.

When Billy died, it was almost instantaneous that he woke up here. He opened his eyes and felt groggy, as if he had been napping. He rubbed his eyes, and his face and his face felt different. His nose and chin were elongated, and his teeth were longer and sharper. His clothes were all black, and when he tried to speak, he had no voice. When Billy looked around at his surroundings, deep down, he knew where he was. When he saw the three demons looking at him from a boulder, he felt a fear that he had never felt before. All Billy could do now was run. The Vampire has been running for a long time.

He was hiding in a crevice at the base of a dormant volcano. He was not tired but confused. *Am I to run like this for eternity? Is this my punishment? Maybe if I defeat them, I can leave.* Billy decided to stay here until the three found him. After what felt like hours, they finally arrived and surrounded him. One to the left had a high vantage point, the second was straight on, and the third was to his right waiting in what looked like an impact crater from a small meteor or volcanic bomb. They just stared at Billy dumbfounded. The demon to the left and up cocked its head. The demon in front of Billy looked up and toward the volcano. The third in the crater turned to run. Billy heard the crunch of rocks. His eyes looked to his right,t and there was a shadow in his peripheral vision. When Billy turned back, he saw the other two demons running off with the third. Something or someone had scared them off.

Billy was too afraid to run. He slowly looked over his right shoulder and saw him. A man with porcelain skin with feather-like wings. He stood twenty feet tall, and his eyes had no pupils but blinked. Lucifer looked down at the Vampire and began to speak in a language that sounded like a mixture of French and Aramaic. The voice booms, and it sends Billy back off his feet. He tries to crawl away backward, but Lucifer takes one step and looks down. In his language, we can only translate one phrase.

"There is no light here," Lucifer says, staring down at Billy.

Billy inches back, but then the ground under him disappears. He is falling down what seems like a well. He falls and hits with a thud. When Billy catches his breath, he looks up the fifty feet and can see Lucifer looking down at him. A boulder is pushed over the hole, and Billy screams soundlessly. The Vampire is now trapped in perpetual darkness for all eternity.

The Day of Wrath is widely known as Judgment Day. God punishes those who have gravely sinned, and their punishments match the offense. Those who have not sinned and have repented are welcomed into Heaven. William Mallek, the Vampire, was sent to the netherworld and met Lucifer. The other in our story is yet to know his fate. Let us see what happens to Michael Phy, the Horseman, on this Day of Wrath.

When Michael awakened, there was a dense fog around him. He lay on rocks and had trouble breathing. When he got to his knees, he, too, felt his face. It was hard and slick. His face was skeletal, and his tattered black hood was stitched to his scalp. His hands were bonelike, and he, too, screamed. Hell is different for everyone, and here Michael's screams are audible. There was a breeze, and some of the fog began to dissipate. Michael could see a shadow in the distant fog. The shape was large and backlit by a bright light. The shape was about ten feet tall and ten feet wide. There were wings. Insect wings. The silhouetted shape was familiar. It was a large Wasp. It turned to the left and then to the front, and then to the right. The wings fluttered at a furious rate. When the Wasp moved, the ground under Michael's feet shook. When the Wasp faced Michael, he did not fear it. He was overcome with a terrible sense of sadness. He, too, knew where he was. The Wasp faced him, and then in an instant, it took off straight up into the sky, and its wings extinguished all the fog left. Michael could now see the barren landscape. It was similar to the landscape Billy saw. Erupting volcanoes on either side, but there were some differences. The sky was gray, not red. The faces of the mountains and volcanoes almost looked like tortured human faces. The only color seemed to come from the brightly lit lava spewing from the volcanoes. Straight ahead, on the edge of eyesight, there were trees or what looked like trees. They were, in fact, large black vines with jagged thorns.

Out of this tangled mess comes a figure. Michael can only see that it is big and running

222

toward him. Michael turns to run himself. Lava bombs begin reigning down all around him, and a terrible yell from the thing chasing him is heard. Michael runs faster but trips and falls to the ground. When he turns to look, this Beast is upon him. Satan has many forms and names. Michael can only assume this is the Beast. Blood-stained skin, with a serpent tongue and fireballs for eyes. Eight feet tall, slender, and dressed like a monster from long ago. The Beast stands over the Horseman. He also begins to speak in a language that is garbled and heinous. It is something from Beelzebub. Horseman stands and faces the Beast. The Beast then lets out a terrible high-pitched scream. Horseman charges the Beast and bounces off him. He rises again and charges in with a shot to the center of the monster. The Beast reaches down, grabs Horseman by the throat, and tosses him ten feet back. The Beast speaks again, and the deciphered translation is the same.

"There is no light here."

The Beast looks to his right and watches a figure come down the face of a volcano. Horseman watches as well and can see that the figure is feminine. She is covered from head to toe in what looks like cracked magma. Underneath her skin of magma is the orange glow of lava. She is almost as tall as the Beast as she stands next to him. Like the three demons, her origin is also unknown. She looks in Horseman's direction even though she has no eyes. In her right hand is a fireball that irradiates light. She shows it to Horseman. She then blows out the fireball in one breath and sends everything into darkness. Almost all sound stops, and all light has been eradicated. The only sound left for the Horseman is his own breathing in his eternal damnation.

Chapter 33

July 3, 1999

It is a Saturday in Seaside Heights. The boardwalk is packed, and the beaches are full of life. The sun shines bright and bounces off Thomas' fishing pole. To his right is his Uncle James, fishing with him on the pier. An American flag flaps in the breeze above them.

"We don't catch much here," Thomas says.

"Sometimes it is good to get out of the house and enjoy a weekend," James replies, looking down at his nephew in a baseball cap.

The waves crash hard on the pier below them, and James knows it will be tough today to catch anything. Not much has changed for James or his family. The times with Thomas become less frequent now that Thomas' parents are taking more time off to see him. James enjoys the times he can share with his nephew.

"Mom was thinking of getting a dog."

"What kind of dog does she want?"

"I'd like a small dog. Like the one that lady has on the beach." Thomas points down to the beach on his left. James peeks over and sees a black woman with a Yorkshire terrier.

"I didn't think they allowed dogs on the beach." James ponders while smiling.

"It's tiny. I bet no one minds."

"I guess not. Do you think we will catch any sharks, Tommy?"

"We might. There are a lot of monsters out there."

"Yes, there are." James starts reeling in his line.

The terrier down on the beach is Princess. Tasha brought her today. It is the first weekend of the summer that Tasha has off. She wanted to get Princess a little exercise considering all the weight the little one had put on from all the generous scraps at the nursing home. Tasha takes a deep breath and can smell and taste the salty ocean air. This summer is going to be a selfish one for Tasha. Too long has she neglected herself. The long hours have taken their toll, and she can feel arthritis settling in her hands and hips. This summer, she will have more days off and more time to find someone. Tasha is ready to at least give love a try one more time.

Up on the north end of the boardwalk is a bench. It is the last bench and is a little more subdued here than the rest of the boardwalk today. Natalia is sitting with her reading glasses on and finishing another romance novel. Paul is to her left and wearing a nasal oxygen cannula. He sits, struggling to breathe. He has aged rapidly over the last year. The death of Laura and his son has taken most of his life. Paul is almost at his end, and his thoughts are random now. He forgets that Natalia is his nurse. He forgets that Laura and his son died. Paul has even forgotten his son's name.

Made in the USA
Middletown, DE
08 April 2023